THE THIRD COMING

OTHER BOOKS BY CÉLESTE PERRINO-WALKER

THE THIRD COMING

CÉLESTE PERRINO-WALKER

Pacific Press® Publishing Association
Nampa, Idaho
Oshawa, Ontario, Canada
www.pacificpress.com

Copyright 2006 by
Pacific Press® Publishing Association
Printed in the United States of America
All rights reserved

Book design by Steve Trapero
Cover photo by Steve Trapero

ISBN: 0-8163-2142-6
ISBN 13: 9780816321421

Additional copies of this book are available by calling toll free 1-800-765-6955 or by visiting <http://www.adventistbookcenter.com>.

06 07 08 09 10 • 5 4 3 2 1

DEDICATION

This book is dedicated to Gary and Rachel Kinne with great affection and gratitude for opening their hearts and home to us when we had no spiritual place to go. This book was conceived during the wonderful hours we spent studying the Bible in their home. We love you guys!

CONTENTS

BOOK ONE:

THE BEGINNING OF THE END

BOOK ONE:
THE BEGINNING OF THE END

CHAPTER ONE

A sharp northeast wind scuttled dead leaves around Maddie Gray's feet as she turned her back on the two-bit diner where she worked from ten each evening until six the next morning. Dull, leaden clouds raced across the sky, spitting snow. Maddie hunched her shoulders and pulled the thin wool coat closer, clutching the fabric to her throat. It was March, and in Vermont, spring was coming in like a lion.

The Midway Diner was located on the edge of the town of Pleasant. If it had been much farther out, Maddie would have had to drive her ancient car to work each day and waste her precious gas allowance. As it was, she barely had time to make it home to change her clothes before rushing to her part-time job as a nurse's aid in a nursing home. The ground had thawed briefly before the latest cold snap, but the mud had since frozen into jagged shapes, and Maddie watched her footing carefully as she walked along the edge of the road into town.

To her right was a sloping driveway leading to a large farmhouse with a big front yard that still had a tire swing hanging from a spreading maple tree that shaded the lawn. Her husband, Daniel, had hung that swing for their children many years ago—a lifetime, it seemed. Maddie passed the driveway and hurried on. The house no longer belonged to her. Another family enjoyed its cheery interior, drank cocoa by the glowing fireplace, and breakfasted in the sunny spot near the French doors that looked onto the patio and the large English garden that had taken Maddie five years to plant exactly the way she wanted.

How she missed that garden.

How she missed that life.

The wind carried off her deep sigh, and she picked up her pace. Her daughter, Lyn, who was fifteen, would be off to school by the time she reached home. Maddie prayed that she'd taken the bus and not hitched a ride with her wild friends—especially that boy, Justin. Though Lyn had always been a sweet, compliant child, one who loved Jesus and enjoyed church activities, Maddie had been prepared to experience concern over her daughter's choice of boyfriends. That was only natural. She hadn't expected to be afraid of them. That was not.

Just thinking of Justin Cooper sent a flash of fear coursing through her that temporarily made her forget that her fingers were getting numb and she could no longer feel her toes inside her crepe-soled shoes. Justin was eighteen, which Maddie objected to on principle alone. But that wasn't what scared her. The boy seemed a caricature of evil. He dressed all in black, his favorite garment being a flowing black trench coat. Tattoos of swastikas and barbed wire decorated his shoulders and forearms. He fairly bristled with metal; his eyebrows, ears, nose, tongue, and bellybutton, which he exposed with a strategically ripped T-shirt, were all pierced. His short hair was greased back flat to his head and usually covered, at least in the winter, with a tight-fitting ski cap. Maddie was a relatively tall woman, thin and angular, but Justin towered over her at what she guessed must be at least six foot three. When he looked at her, his eyes full of contempt, she felt like a bug he was about to squash under his Nazi-style jackboots.

"Please, God," Maddie prayed, her breath a whistle in the wind, "please let Lyn have gone to school on the bus. Keep her safe from Justin."

For some reason Maddie couldn't comprehend and Lyn couldn't explain clearly, Justin fascinated her daughter. She treated the nice boys at church who were interested in her as if they were well-meaning younger brothers to be tolerated and endured. But she hung on Justin's every word. If he snapped his fingers, she'd come running. In one of her painfully sarcastic moments, Maddie had asked Lyn if she'd jump off a bridge at Justin's request. Chillingly, Lyn had said Yes.

Maddie was shivering uncontrollably when she finally reached the dilapidated tenement building where she lived. The long, low building used to be white, but most of the color had worn off, leaving the boards a soft gray flecked with peeling paint. Maddie lived on the second floor in an eight-hundred-square-foot apartment. As she climbed the stairs, they creaked beneath her, and the handrail shook under her fingers.

What she really needed was a long soak in a hot bath, but the water in the apartment was warm at best, no matter how long you ran it. Instead, she put the kettle on for a cup of tea to warm her up while she shed her coat and took her shoes off to rub some circulation back into her feet.

"Have you got any money, Ma?"

Maddie clutched at her chest and uttered a shriek of surprise. She was so startled that she nearly fell off the wobbly kitchen chair on which she was sitting,

"Whatsa matter? Weren't you expecting to see me? I still live here, ya know."

Her son, Brian, who for all intents and purposes had left home three years before, when he turned sixteen, had materialized in the doorway between the kitchen and the hallway that led to the cramped bedrooms. Maddie's mind raced. If he was asking for money, surely he hadn't found where she'd hidden it. Or had he found it and hoped for more?

Brian looked even worse than the last time she'd seen him, maybe a month ago. His normally thin frame was gaunt; his cheeks scratchy as sandpaper and hollow as dippers. A shabby sweater hung loosely around him, the tattered sleeves covering his forearms and hiding the recent tracks of needle marks Maddie was certain were there. Brian was a heroin addict and only showed up when he was desperate and needed money for a fix.

Brian's eyes were bright, and a fine film of sweat stood out on his blanched forehead. "Well? Have you got any money or not? I haven't got all day."

"It's good to see you, Brian," Maddie said, stalling for time, praying under her breath for the wisdom to know what to do.

"Money, Ma. I need money." Brian's voice was rising. Soon he would be hysterical, or, worse, violent. "I know what you're thinking. It's not for drugs; not this time. I just need some money so I can get out of this hell-hole."

"This isn't hell, son," Maddie said slowly, gauging his reaction. "This is a fallen, dark place, but here we still have access to God. Hell is the absence of God."

Brian whimpered, then erupted. "Don't talk to me about God!"

"But, Brian . . ." Maddie's voice was soft, tender; her eyes filled suddenly with tears as she remembered her son as a small boy, when their family was intact in happy times. Where had that smiling, joy-filled child gone? Was he still alive inside this shell of a disappointed, bitter man-child? She reached out as if to take him in her arms as she had done when he was small and had skinned his knee, but he snarled and pulled away from her.

"I know you've got a stash of money here, Ma. Give it to me, or so help me, I'll . . ." Brian's words trailed away as a heavy fist pounded on the door.

"Police! Open up!"

"You haven't seen me, Ma," Brian hissed as he dived for the hallway.

Shaken, Maddie made her way to the front door and pulled it open. Two police officers stood on the threshold. Maddie quaked with fear for her son, and she wondered what he had done to bring the law to her door.

"We have an arrest warrant for Brian Gray. Is he here?" The officer fixed her with a cold and merciless eye. Maddie knew she couldn't lie. Not even to save her son, who, God help him, must have done something very, very wrong.

"He's—" she began, but at that moment Brian charged across the room and grabbed her from behind.

"Get back or I'll shoot her," he warned, putting the cold steel barrel of a pistol to her temple and daring the police to challenge him. Maddie closed her eyes. That she could die in the next few moments at the hands of her son didn't concern her half as much as the thought of those she'd leave behind. How would they manage without her? What would become of Lyn, who was being pulled toward the darkness, away from the light? Who would visit her husband, Daniel, in prison? Would the police shoot Brian if he killed her? The thoughts raced through her head like bullets being shot in rapid succession from Brian's gun.

The police officers held up their hands and stepped back from the door. "Easy, son," one said. "Don't do anything foolish."

Brian laughed harshly. "That's rich. You wouldn't be here if I hadn't done anything foolish. Now just get in your little car and make like you were never here."

"You won't get away, son. Turn yourself in now before you get in any worse trouble."

"Don't call me 'son'!" Brian screamed. Bits of foam spattered against Maddie's cheek from the force of his words. "Get out of here! Go!"

The officers backed slowly down the stairs, keeping their eyes trained on Brian and Maddie standing in the doorway. When they had gotten into their patrol car and driven away around a corner, Brian bolted past Maddie and clattered down the stairs. The feeble railing splintered and gave way as he careened against it. He fell hard onto the frozen ground below and for a moment lay stunned. Then he picked himself up and limped away. He hadn't made it halfway across the next lot before Maddie heard the howl of sirens. Lurching around a corner, Brian was lost from sight.

It wasn't until cruisers screeched into the parking lot and spilled police officers who charged up the stairs to check on her that Maddie realized she was standing like an idiot with the door open in the freezing cold. But she wasn't dead.

BOOK ONE:
THE BEGINNING OF THE END

CHAPTER TWO

Maddie arrived at work an hour late and stopped by her supervisor's office to explain. The woman was kind. Her only concern was for Maddie's safety, which caused Maddie to begin weeping for the first time that whole dreadful morning. The older woman patted her on the shoulder and silently passed her a tissue. "There, there, everything will be all right now." Her blue eyes were sympathetic, and her voice, gentle.

Maddie wanted to pour out her concern for her son, but she knew it would be inappropriate and misconstrued. So she bit her tongue and tried to regain control of her emotions. The woman's next words confirmed her intuition. "I'm sure the police have him safely in custody by this time. Don't worry, my dear. He won't be able to harm you now."

"Thank you," Maddie whispered hoarsely. The thought of her son languishing in some cold jail along with her husband did nothing to comfort her. But then perhaps that's what Brian needed. Perhaps he had to go where he couldn't get any lower for God to show him the way up again. As He had with her husband, Daniel.

Maddie worked her shift mechanically. Already tired from working all night, she longed for sleep. Her hands performed each task, but her mind wandered above it all, hazy with fatigue. Even the strong smells of urine and body odor didn't penetrate her mental fog. She had no idea how she managed to get through the rest of her partial shift, but she thanked God for helping her.

"See you tomorrow, dearie," an elderly woman said in her scratchy voice as Maddie pulled on her coat for the walk home.

Maddie smiled at the woman, fluttering her hand in a wave. "God willing," she agreed.

Sometimes Lyn came home from school to have lunch with her. The thought quickened her weary steps. The nursing home was located only six blocks from her apartment, and the walk took about ten minutes if she hurried. She longed for her bed. After about five hours' sleep, she usually woke to spend her evenings tidying up and hand washing a few small articles of clothing that she didn't want to leave for the weekly trek to the laundromat. If Lyn was going to be home and Maddie had enough energy, she did a little cooking for their late dinner. If she didn't have the energy or Lyn was out with her friends, she took out something she'd made ahead and frozen.

If Lyn was home tonight when Maddie returned from her weekly prison visit, Maddie would skip her chores and offer to make them a pot of tea. They could sit at the worn Formica-topped table and chat. They hadn't done that in ages. Maybe Lyn would even agree to let Maddie read her a few chapters of the Bible as they used to do when Lyn was a child. Later, Lyn would study her homework in the kitchen while Maddie made them something nourishing, like a hearty stew. Something that would warm them inside and out.

But the apartment was deserted when Maddie arrived. Instead of Lyn, she found a note on the table. "Mom, going with Justin after school. Lyn." No "love." No hint of when she would return. No idea of where they were going. Nothing. Heavy-hearted, Maddie cleaned the kitchen, washing dishes left over from breakfast and some Lyn apparently had dirtied during her brief sojourn at home before she'd left with Justin.

Then Maddie tidied up the living room, shifting to the dirty clothes hamper articles of clothing Lyn had left on the floor, and returning the few magazines and books she possessed to the bookcase, from which they had somehow escaped—possibly disturbed by Brian in his search for money. When she was finished, she pulled on her coat again and retrieved her keys for the drive to the state penitentiary, where she'd make her weekly visit to her husband.

The old car chugged and lurched as she drove the six miles out of town to the squat brick building surrounded by a tall wire fence topped with rolls of razor wire that bristled against the rural setting. Her husband, Daniel, had been incarcerated for the past ten years, following a conviction for first-degree murder.

In their former life, in happier times, Daniel had owned a thriving auto-repair shop. He was a gifted mechanic and had been doing well. At first, he drank only occasionally. But as his success increased, so did his drinking, until he was out of control. When he'd discovered that an employee had been cheating him, he'd killed the man in a drunken rage.

THE THIRD COMING

Sentenced to death for his crime, Daniel spent his days on death row searching the Bible for the answers he thought he should already have had. There he met God, who changed him.

Maddie had visited the prison so often that the guards frequently joked that she should be on staff. In fact, in the past they had asked her to study with some of the inmates who'd requested Bible studies. But they hadn't asked lately. Things had begun to change. The air was filled with a new kind of tension that set Maddie's teeth on edge, though she wasn't quite sure why.

Daniel was waiting for her in the visitor's room when she arrived. A shiver ran down her spine when she thought that he'd have been waiting for her in vain if Brian had made good his threat that morning. Daniel noticed her anxiety right away and took her hand—the only contact they were permitted, and that because of the guard's leniency.

"What's wrong? Are you OK?" His dark eyes were worried above the bushy black beard.

"I'm OK, but I don't know about Brian." Quickly she told him what had happened.

"Did they catch him?"

"Not yet."

Maddie sighed. Just before she'd left the apartment that afternoon, a police officer had called to warn her that they hadn't caught her son and she'd be wise to spend the next few nights with a friend just in case. She'd called her best friend, Jean King, who had agreed to let Maddie and Lyn spend the night. But she'd have to wait until Lyn returned home to tell her.

"Let's pray about it," Daniel urged. He bowed his head.

"Heavenly Father, we beseech Thee to watch over our boy, Brian. He's searching for Thee, O God. Reveal Thyself to him. Protect him and the police officers who are searching for him. Give him the strength to turn himself in, and keep him from any further bloodshed. We ask Thee, God of heaven, to save us from the darkness of this life and bring us to the joy of Thy salvation. Forgive us when we trespass against Thee. In the name of Thy holy and flawless Son. Amen."

Maddie loved the way her husband prayed in such formal, King James English. He'd learned to pray that way, he'd told her, from the elderly man who'd given him Bible studies at the jail. There was something in the formality of the words that comforted her. They washed over her like poetry, and she felt as though he were singing the words to God.

When Daniel looked up, tears wet his cheeks and ran into his beard. "It's my fault this is going on. If I'd been there to help you raise him, none of this would be happening. We'd still be in our house, all of us together. You wouldn't have had to move to that broken-down excuse for an apartment and work all hours just to keep a roof over your head. I'm so, so sorry that I let you down, Maddie."

"I know, Daniel," Maddie said kindly. "You can't blame yourself. Brian might still be in this predicament even if things had gone on as they were. We don't know. Only God can know how he would have turned out. Only God can know his heart even now. Brian could have killed me today, but he didn't. That says something about his heart, right? It can't be completely hard yet."

Daniel wiped his eyes with the back of his hand, and Maddie realized with a start how old and tired he looked. There were deep hollows beneath his eyes, and for the first time she noticed how bony his wrists were. She wondered if they were starving him.

"How's my girl?" Daniel asked, trying to smile, expecting good news about Lyn.

Maddie bit her lip, wishing she could tell Daniel a little white lie. Wishing she could tell him all the things she wanted to be true—that Lyn was dating a nice boy who respected her, that she was attending church regularly and participating in the activities, that she was the same bright, cheerful child Daniel remembered. But she couldn't.

"I'm worried about her," she finally admitted. "That boy she's so taken with scares me. Since she met him, she's changed so much. I hardly recognize her anymore. She's seldom home, and when she is, she's sullen and withdrawn. Her whole personality has changed in just the last month."

"Forbid her to see him," Daniel entreated. His hands gripped hers like a man drowning in a sea of fear.

"I can't. I mean, I tried that, but it didn't work. She just sneaks off to be with him. A couple of nights she didn't come home, and I know she was with him. But what can I do?"

"Oh, God, my children are deserting Thee," Daniel moaned, covering his anguished face with his hands. "The sins of their father are being visited upon them. I cannot bear this grief!"

Maddie tried to reach across the table to put her arms around her husband, but the guard in the corner cleared his throat meaningfully. So, she simply sat and stared at Daniel wretchedly, unable to offer any comfort. "Daniel, please," she implored, "our God is mighty and powerful to save. Our children are in His hands. We must trust Him. If we can't, who can we trust?"

Eventually, Daniel's sobs subsided, and Maddie glanced anxiously toward the large clock. They must part soon. Maddie hated their visit to end in grief and pain.

"Daniel, look at me. God saved me, and He saved you. He can save our children. We need to put them in His hands. He can hold them. *He can.* I believe that."

Daniel nodded wordlessly. With dismay, Maddie saw the guard approach and put his hand on Daniel's elbow. "Time to go," he said softly.

Daniel rose, but he made no move to leave. Instead, he looked at Maddie, his gaze intense with sorrow and longing. "See you next week?" he asked.

Maddie bobbed her head, not willing to trust her voice. But when Daniel had shambled as far as the door, she called after him, "God keep you, Daniel! I love you!" She saw him halt for a moment and half turn. Then the guard urged him forward, and he was gone.

CHAPTER THREE

Lyn came home after Maddie had eaten supper. Maddie had packed her own things and, beginning to panic, was in Lyn's room trying to decide what to pack for her so they could leave the moment Lyn arrived. She hadn't been able to get a wink of sleep, so she had called her boss at the diner to tell him what had happened and to say that she needed some time off to get her life sorted out. Her boss wasn't happy about it, but Maddie never called in sick and never took personal time, so he agreed Maddie could have the next two nights off.

Maddie vaguely heard the door open, but the sound didn't register. Exhausted, she was staring stupidly at the box that she had just pulled from Lyn's trashcan. It was the empty packaging from a pregnancy test kit. Her eyes moved, as though drawn, from the kit to a white plastic stick on the dresser. She hadn't noticed it before.

Pregnant.

Her daughter was pregnant.

"Mom! What are you doing in my room?" Lyn shrieked from the doorway, her eyes blazing. She threw herself across the room and snatched the box out of Maddie's hands as if she could undo the damage that had just been done.

Maddie gaped at her daughter. "You're pregnant."

"Duh! You don't have to be a brain surgeon to figure that one out, do you?" Lyn spat. "What gives you the right to go through my trash?"

Maddie straightened up and felt a little spark of energy inside. "I am your mother, Lyndell. This is my house. I can go through whatever I want: the laundry, the garbage, or even the lint in the carpet if I like."

Lyn deflated slightly, and Maddie knew that no matter how far Lyn had strayed, inside, she was still just a kid who wanted to please.

"Why are you in my room?" Lyn asked again, slightly less belligerently.

"I was trying to pack for you. The police have asked us to spend the night somewhere else because we might not be safe here."

"Not safe? Why isn't our home safe?"

As Maddie told her about Brian, Lyn transformed from the defiant teenager she was trying to be into the timid little girl she had always been. Her mouth worked, and her face crumpled. "But I don't understand," she said. "Why would Brian want to hurt you? He loves you, Mommy. I know he does." She seemed genuinely bewildered.

Maddie didn't have time to go into further details. They could discuss Brian later, when they were safe. The longer they lingered, the greater the chance Brian would catch them at home, and she didn't want to expose Lyn to his violence.

"Come on, honey," she urged. "What do you want to bring to Jean's? We might have to stay for a couple of days."

Between them, they packed a bag for Lyn. Not a word was said about the baby—about all that a baby would mean in their lives. Lyn's pregnancy hung between them like a dark and frightening cloud.

At the thought of all that had befallen her that day, Maddie felt as drained and empty as if she'd been opened up and poured out onto the stained carpet. *How, God, will I endure unless You give me strength?* she asked silently.

No, she thought, *not to* endure, *but to* prevail. *God doesn't call us to endure. He calls us to triumph. When sin happened, He didn't patch up the hearts of human beings; He re-created them.*

These thoughts filled Maddie with a kind of deep contentment—not at her circumstances, but at her place in her circumstances. It was her place to do what God commanded. It was His responsibility to make gold from the dross of her life. She figured God was up to the challenge, and He didn't need her help, only her willingness to obey.

They drove in silence to the other side of town, where Jean and her husband lived in a small, neat house with a postage-stamp lawn surrounded by a white picket fence. Maddie parked her car next to Jean's SUV, and taking Lyn's bag as well as her own, she made her way slowly up the walk as Lyn dragged reluctantly along behind her.

Jean threw open the door of the little house, and light spilled onto the stoop. A gush of warmth from inside, scented with gingerbread and applesauce, washed over Maddie, and she forgot for a moment the circumstances that had brought her, bag and baggage, to Jean's door.

"Come in; come in! It's a three-dog-night out tonight for sure," Jean said, shooing them into the house and taking the bags from Maddie. "Go right on into the kitchen," she called over her shoulder as she trundled the bags down the hallway to her spare bedroom. "I've made us some cookies and mulled cider. That should take the chill off. Ernie's gone to work down at the plant. It's just us chicks for the night."

Maddie wandered gratefully into the kitchen, a place where she and Jean had spent many happy hours cooking together, having tea, and just being friends. Lyn stubbornly plopped down on the couch and slouched there with a frown on her face. Maddie ignored her. This was hard on all of them.

As Maddie pulled a stool up to the counter and reached for a cookie, the feeling that something was vastly different about the kitchen dawned on her. The refrigerator was new, as were the dishwasher and the stove. In fact, most of the appointments were new—from the countertops to the cabinets and the tile on the floor.

"You've redecorated!" she exclaimed as Jean entered the kitchen.

Jean fluttered her hands. "Yes, well, a little."

"Little?" Maddie couldn't identify a single old appliance. "You had to have saved a long time. You must be so pleased."

"Oh, I am. I surely am," Jean said. She seemed reluctant to talk any more about it, so Maddie let the subject drop.

"Have you heard any more news from the police?" Jean asked, dropping her voice.

"No. They said they'd call the minute they knew anything good or bad. I'm so worried about Brian."

"Poor Brian," Jean said, shaking her head, her long salt-and-pepper ringlets bouncing like springs framing her big, round face. "I feel bad for that boy. He always was missing something, wasn't he? You could just see him look for it. Well, he found it in the wrong place, that's for sure."

Maddie nodded miserably. "I feel like such a failure," she said.

"Don't," Jean replied firmly. "As parents, our responsibility is to bring our children up to know and obey God. What they do after that is between them and God. Look at Adam and Eve. God created them, and when He turned His back for a minute, they went off and got into trouble. If having

God for a parent isn't enough insurance to prevent kids from taking the wrong path, then I guess we can't expect to do any better."

"I know. But I can't help feeling that I failed him somehow. Maybe if I had paid more attention when he started getting into trouble—"

"You were working," Jean interrupted. "There was only so much you could do. The way things are in the world today, it's a wonder any of us make it through. I always said we should never have gone to war with Iraq—not with all that oil at stake. Some idiot over there was bound to torch the whole business. And I was right. Now look at us, rationing gas. It's absurd, a country as wealthy as ours rationing its gasoline. And all the while, that oil burning up over there, filling the air with that black smoke. I tell you, it's shameful. Now it's making the weather go all haywire on us. Why, do you know it rained frogs in Albuquerque yesterday?"

"Frogs?" Maddie said stupidly. "Real frogs?"

"Real frogs." Jean's mouth puckered, registering her own disgust and disbelief. "Practically a plague of frogs is what the television said. What's next? Locusts?

"And the riots! Why practically every night on the news, Ernie and I hear about some new riot. I know you don't have a television, honey, but I swear it's the truth. The looting and violence—why, it makes me afraid to go out of my house."

"But, Jean," Maddie protested, "there's been no looting here."

Jean wagged her head back and forth dolefully like the clapper of a giant bell tolling approaching doom. "It's only a matter of time, my dear, only a matter of time. Just because we are fortunate to live up here in the middle of nowhere doesn't mean we'll escape God's wrath. That's what this is, you know. God is pouring out His wrath as a judgment on humankind for their sinning ways. Mark my words. We're not safe here either. Sooner or later, we'll be affected."

"Jean," Maddie said gently, "think about what you're saying. Why would God punish the good along with the wicked?"

"Don't bad things happen to good people?" Jean pointed out logically.

"Yes, but God doesn't make them happen."

"Well," Jean huffed, "there's no law says you have to agree with me. We all have our own interpretation of the Bible. We can't go around judging each other on theological points now, can we?"

Maddie sat in an uncomfortable silence while Jean busied herself refreshing their cider and rearranging the cookies. Then their talk turned to other, less controversial subjects, and when Maddie noticed the time, it was after eleven. "I really should be getting to bed," she yawned.

"I put you both in the spare room," Jean said. "Sleep in as long as you like."

"I have to be at the nursing home by seven," Maddie said.

"There's an alarm clock on the nightstand," Jean said. "Ernie comes in around seven, but I'll have breakfast going before that."

Maddie hugged her friend. She felt safe and cared for in her solid embrace.

"Thank you for taking us in, Jean."

"That's what friends are for, honey," Jean said brightly.

They found Lyn asleep on the couch in front of the television. Jean turned it off and suggested they cover her with quilts and let her sleep.

Later, as Maddie lay between the crisp sheets, she thought about what Jean had said. "I know You don't punish the good along with the wicked, God," she murmured sleepily. "I know that You watch over and protect Your people. Watch over us all tonight and keep us safe spiritually if not physically. Amen."

As Maddie drifted off to sleep, she dreamed of dark angels and light angels fighting as they swirled around the earth, which spun crazily on its axis and all the while drew nearer and nearer to the edge of a fathomless precipice.

CHAPTER FOUR

Maddie woke the next morning not to the shrill of the alarm clock but to the unmistakable aroma of eggs. She hadn't eaten an egg in at least six months; not since the government had discovered that 80 percent of the nation's laying hens were infected with some disease related to mad cow disease and had ordered them all slaughtered. Eggs were something only the very rich could afford, if they could find them.

She pulled on her worn flannel robe and tied it as she made her way down the dark hallway. As she reached the living room, a loud boom startled her. Outside the picture window, a jagged fork of lightning split the sky. A severe wind shook the house and pelted large drops of rain against the windows. Maddie wondered if spring were merely being fickle or if this was more of the disastrous weather Jean had told her about.

"Weird weather," Jean mourned dolefully as Maddie entered the kitchen. "It's as warm as June outside."

"That's March for you: In like a lion, out like a lamb," Maddie said, quoting the old axiom.

"That's no lamb," Jean snorted. "That's a monster." Another crash sounded, and they both jumped.

On the table were piles of toast and eggs, boxes of cereal, and a pitcher of freshly squeezed orange juice.

"Jean, what a feast!" Maggie said. "You didn't have to go to any trouble for us!"

"It's no trouble." Jean seemed pleased with the compliment. "Ernie likes a hearty breakfast when he gets home from work. Then he falls into a stupor and sleeps it off most of the day. It's really our only big meal. I just snack during the day, and when Ernie gets up, we have a light supper."

"But the eggs!" Maddie was aghast. There had to be nearly a dozen, scrambled and fluffy, piled up in a bowl and steaming their pleasant aroma throughout the kitchen. "I'm afraid to eat a single mouthful, knowing what they must have cost you. Where did you ever find them?"

"I have my ways," Jean said smugly. "It's not impossible to find eggs; you just have to know where to look."

"But the cost!"

"Ernie and I have a little salted away. We've been frugal for years. Now we like to treat ourselves."

Maddie couldn't remember a time when Jean and Ernie had fit even a loose definition of frugal. In good times, they had done a lot of traveling, bought top-of-the-line cars, and indulged expensive tastes. Maybe when they had sold their large house after their children moved away and bought this smaller place, they had a fair amount of profit to put away.

Maddie pulled up a chair and then frowned. "Where's Lyn?"

"She left already. A boy came and picked her up early this morning. I don't mind telling you, Maddie, I didn't like the looks of that boy. Not one bit."

Maddie swallowed hard, her appetite suddenly gone. "No," she said slowly. "I'm afraid of him myself."

"I'm really surprised at you allowing Lyn to see a boy like that, what with all the nice boys at church who are interested in her."

"I don't have any choice. I forbade her to see him, but she does it anyway. I'm afraid if I come down any harder, she'll just leave."

"Let her!" Jean said hotly. "Let her leave! She'll come crawling back to you, mark my words."

"There's something else . . ."

Was it right to share her concerns about Lyn's pregnancy?

Jean, who had always seemed keenly attuned to gossip, sat down quickly and pulled her chair closer to Maddie. "Yes? Go on."

"About Lyn . . ." Something in Maddie's heart urged her to go no further. "She's, well, she's really upset about Brian," she finished lamely.

Jean snorted. "Is that all? I expect she *should* be upset that her brother nearly blew her mother's head off yesterday. I guess that's upsetting all right."

Clearly disappointed that she wouldn't be learning anything juicier, Jean pushed her chair away and began to heap a plate with breakfast items. Just as she finished, Ernie walked in the door and took it from her.

"Thanks, Doll," he said, pecking his wife's cheek as he passed.

"Don't mention it," she returned dryly. "That was for Maddie, by the way."

Ernie pinched a large clump of eggs from the plate and dropped it into his mouth. "You don't say. Sorry, Maddie. Help yourself. There's plenty more."

Jean's hands went to her hips, and she fixed her husband with a narrow, disapproving gaze. "Aren't you going to say hello to our guest? Where *are* your manners?"

"Hullo, Maddie," Ernie said obligingly. "Sleep well, did you?"

"Very well, thanks." Maddie hid a smile. Jean and Ernie seemed to do nothing but bicker, but she knew they would do anything for each other.

"Quite some weather we're having," Ernie ventured, chewing thoughtfully. Thunder punctuated his sentence. He gave her an encouraging smile. He'd never been much of a conversationalist, and Maddie was sorry he had to put himself out to entertain company during breakfast.

"Unusual," Maddie agreed. "Very good eggs," she added. "Such a treat."

"Hmm? Yes, well, only get them a couple times a week now, but still better than most, I imagine."

Better than most by a long shot, Maddie wanted to say, but she bit her tongue. That would be some way to repay Jean and Ernie's generous hospitality! Ruefully, she finished the last few bites, relishing the taste and knowing it would be a long time before she had eggs again.

"It's time I got to work," she said. "It's a little farther to walk from here than it is from home."

"Nonsense," Ernie said. "Jean will drive you."

"I certainly shall," Jean said, leaving no room for argument.

"Thank you." Maddie blinked her eyes rapidly to dispel the tears of gratitude that threatened to spill down her cheeks. "I'll go and get ready."

The day passed quickly. When she was on her usual meager rations, Maddie's stomach began to growl shortly before she left work. Today, however, she enjoyed the sensation of pleasant fullness so long that she could hardly believe the entire morning had passed. As she struggled to get her umbrella open before stepping outside to search the parking lot for Jean, who had promised to pick her up, she was interrupted by a uniformed police officer.

"Madeline Gray?" he inquired.

"Yes, I'm Maddie Gray," she replied. There was something in his grave face, something in the way he removed his cap and stood before her like a boy before the principal's desk, something in the ashen color of his skin that told her he bore her no good tidings.

"Mrs. Gray, I'm Officer Ryan. I'm afraid I have some upsetting news. A few hours ago, an officer in Brattleboro responded to a call from a motorist who was concerned about a car traveling at an excessive speed down the interstate. The officer chased the car, but the driver lost control and slammed through a guardrail into a cliff on the side of the highway.

"The pursuing officer attempted to pull the driver from the wreckage, but the car exploded, and both the driver and the officer were killed. Dental records confirm that the driver was your son, Brian Gray."

Maddie felt her heart stop. She felt sure it had stopped. But she didn't die. She didn't even faint. She stood instead like a statue of a woman who had just lost her son. Yet she hadn't just lost him—not really. Brian had been leaving for years. The only difference now was that he wouldn't be coming home again.

Had he made his peace with God before he crashed into the cliff? Maddie wanted to know that. But more than anything, she wanted him to have done it. She wanted him to have been right with God before he died.

"I'm so sorry for your loss, Officer Ryan," she said, and she reached out and placed her hand on his hands, which were twisting his cap.

Ryan regarded her with worried eyes. "Ma'am?" he said, looking puzzled—as though he were watching a horse run backwards or hearing a dog meow. "Are you OK? Maybe you should sit down."

"I'm not OK. I don't think that's an option when you lose a child. But I will be OK because I have God to lean on. I'm so very sorry about the loss of your fellow officer. It was very courageous of him to try to help my son. 'Greater love has no man . . .' "

At this, her voice faded, and she was sure that if she went on, she would break down and cry, and she wanted to save that for the privacy of her own room, her own room in her own shabby little apartment.

"God be with you, Officer Ryan."

THE THIRD COMING

Without bothering to open her umbrella, Maddie stepped out into the storm and walked across the parking lot to where Jean was waiting and peering anxiously out of the rain-slurried windshield for a glimpse of her. As Maddie woodenly climbed into the car, she felt like an old, old woman who'd been alive since the dawn of time.

"Take me home, Jean—to my home," she said.

Jean's brow wrinkled in worry. "But Brian—" she began.

"—is dead," Maddie finished, laying her head back against the head-rest and squeezing her eyes shut before the tears could spill. "Take me home. Please take me home."

BOOK ONE:
THE BEGINNING OF THE END

CHAPTER FIVE

A police officer went to the penitentiary to tell Daniel about Brian's death, so Maddie was spared having to break the news to her husband that their only son had died while running from the police. Lyn apparently heard about her brother's death on the news or from a friend. Jean told Maddie later that the girl had simply shown up, collected her things, and driven off with "that boy." She hadn't been home since, and Maddie was worried about her.

"God, what am I going to do about Lyn?" Maddie asked over and over. No answer came, but Maddie knew that God cared and that He knew what was best even if she didn't. Struggling with grief, she was content to leave the matter in His hands.

Because of the manner of Brian's death, Maddie made as little of his funeral service as she could, not that she had much choice. Her own church had no building. And she'd tried repeatedly to reach her pastor but got no answer when she called his home. In the end, she managed to scrape together enough money to entice a priest to conduct the simple service. It was a quiet memorial with only a few family members in attendance. She had Brian's remains cremated because, as the undertaker had bluntly put it, there wasn't enough left of Brian to do anything else.

Lyn, red-eyed and tearful, showed up near the end of the service and stood in the rear of the chapel with Justin, who surveyed the proceedings with disdain. Prison authorities refused to allow Daniel a supervised leave of absence to attend his son's funeral, but he sent a few words to be read during the service.

Maddie didn't know the priest who conducted the service, and he hadn't known Brian and wouldn't have cared if he had. His voice was monotone as he dished out the standard funeral fare. Maddie bit her tongue to keep from correcting him when he spoke about Brian as having "strayed from the path of righteousness" and hoped that "God would have mercy on his misguided soul." His comments made it clear that not only did he question the advisability of admitting someone of Brian's character into heaven at all, but he also highly doubted the probability of it, an eleventh-hour change of heart notwithstanding.

The priest spoke of the "punishment" heaped upon the damned by a God anxious to defend His holy name, and he alluded to his belief that the prayers of the righteous could somehow avert this punishment even now if they were fervent and earnest enough. He said they could speed the deceased out of purgatory, where he certainly was now suffering if he was lucky. Maddie wanted to cry out that the priest didn't know her God, but etiquette kept her quiet as he wound down his sermonette and stepped from the lectern, apparently satisfied that he'd been as fair to the deceased as was necessary.

Only Jean stood with Maddie out in the windswept graveyard as they lowered the small box containing Brian's ashes into the cold earth. Tears streaming down her face, Maddie clutched at Jean's coat and sobbed bitterly. She would have given anything, anything to know that her son had died like the thief on the cross, his heart right with God. She would have forfeited her own salvation for such an assurance, but in her heart, she dreaded the truth.

"I know he would have come around eventually," she wept. "I just know it. But now it's too late. If only he hadn't run away. If only he had gone to prison. I could have talked to him there. Daniel might have been able to talk to him. At least, he would have had a chance. What chance does he have now?"

No one answered her anguished question. Jean simply patted her back and smoothed her snarled hair, searching her face with worried eyes. "Maddie, you need to take care of yourself. Brian may be gone, but you're still here, and you can't let yourself go on like this. Have you been eating?"

Trust Jean to think of temporal things when what Maddie really needed was spiritual assurance. "I don't know," she answered wearily. "I don't care."

"Tsk, tsk, you must start caring. Let me take care of you until you're back on your feet and this terrible ordeal is behind you."

Maddie knew that the terrible ordeal would never be behind her. It would always pierce her heart like the thorns of Christ's crown. How could she think of anything else when the salvation of her only son was in question? She allowed Jean to mother and fuss. She allowed her to buy bags of the best food available and return her to her shabby apartment. But when Jean had gone, she curled into a little ball wrapped in every quilt she could find and cried into her pillow as day turned to night and back into day. When she finally stopped crying and her eyes dried, her chest hurt from the force of her sobs, but she had a new hope in her heart.

Even if Brian had died unsaved, he still might change his mind, Maddie thought. *Surely, sinners who really wanted to repent must have the opportunity to do so before their final end.* And Maddie was sure that given one more chance, Brian would change his mind. She eagerly mentioned this to Daniel on her next visit.

"When the New Jerusalem returns, there might be a chance for anyone who repents to join the redeemed in the city," she said. "They might have a second chance. God loves us all so much, surely He would allow a sinner to repent even at the eleventh hour."

Daniel, who seemed to have aged ten years in a week, pondered this idea before nodding slowly. "That might be true," he agreed. "I hope with all my heart that you're right. I blame myself entirely for Brian's failings as a son and as a person. I wasn't there to do my job as his father. I taught him by my example to defy authority, so how could I expect him to act in any other way? The guilt I feel is so heavy that what's about to happen is almost a relief."

Daniel reached out to take Maddie's hands, shifting his eyes quickly to the guard, who gazed steadfastly away from them. "Madeline, there's something you should know."

Maddie was instantly alert. Her intuition, sharpened by fresh pain, sensed that more was fast approaching.

"What is it?"

"They've stepped up the executions for the prisoners who are Christians. Five were executed in the last week alone."

She frowned. "But that's too unusual not to have made the news."

"It won't make the news," Daniel said. "They don't want it in the news. Even the guards here won't talk about it. But it's happening all the same. I don't know how many are in front of me. Our Bible studies and the men's ministries we do have resulted in so many conversions in the past few months that the number of Christian prisoners has skyrocketed. But it's only a matter of time. My number is bound to come up soon."

"I'll appeal," Maddie said instantly as the horrible truth dawned on her. "I'll appeal to the governor. I'm sure he has no idea what the warden is doing. He'll put a stop to it."

Daniel reached out a hand and stroked her cheek. "Maddie, Maddie, don't you see? It's the end of the line for earth. I may go before you, but it won't be long now before we're all together again in the earth made new. I don't need you to appeal to our crooked governor; I need you to be strong and promise me you'll look after our daughter. I want all of us, our whole family, including Brian, to walk the streets of heaven together. With God, all things are possible, remember?"

Maddie's tears anointed Daniel's fingers as he caressed her cheek a moment longer before the guard noticed the unauthorized touch and purposefully approached them. Maddie wanted to clutch at Daniel like a drowning woman and howl her grief, but she clenched her hands and summoned every remaining ounce of self-control. Daniel's last glimpse of her would not be that of a woman in the throes of a mental breakdown. He would see her bravely hoping with him for the reunification of their family. He would carry this picture with him until they put an end to his life. Nothing would make her leave him with less. If he was brave enough to face death, she was brave enough to face life.

Before the guard reached them, Daniel quickly leaned forward and kissed her, his rough beard scratching her face. "I love you, Maddie," he whispered against her lips as the guard jerked him back. "I'll see you soon."

"I love you, Daniel," Maddie said, fighting to maintain control of her voice. She forced herself to smile, hoping her lips would obey though they were numb. She watched him being pulled toward the door and noticed that though his shoulders were stooped as though bowed beneath the weight of grief, there was a lightness in his step that bore witness to the hope he carried. When Daniel disappeared through the door without looking back, Maddie turned to make her way out of the prison.

As usual, she stopped at the front desk to be buzzed out. The guard on duty there had always been friendly with her and usually indulged in some light banter. She asked him if he had heard anything about the executions taking place at the prison. His face flattened and the light went out of his eyes. "I don't know what you're talking about," he said. Then his eyes narrowed, and he searched her face sharply. Dropping his voice to a near-whisper, he confided, "I'll only say this once: Never, never mention this subject to anyone again. Ever. It's not good for your health. Or mine."

The guard pressed the buzzer, releasing the door, and Maddie stepped into the lobby of the prison and made her way outside, her thoughts whirling in sickening circles. What if Daniel and Jean were right? What if this was the end? What if Jesus was coming soon? Had she been so caught up in her crazy life that she had neglected to keep watch and missed the signs?

Suddenly, Maddie felt ill. Her children's salvation was her first concern, yet it struck her that she herself had slowly drifted away from church. When the congregation lost its building, the members had started meeting in each other's houses. She'd lost track of the schedule months ago, and since she didn't have a phone, no one could call to keep in touch either. Without access to a television, only snatches of radio reports and no newspaper or Internet because of the expense, she'd been scraping by on a superficial level, consumed with her own problems, completely unaware that all around her the world was rapidly changing. So it was quite possible that not much time remained.

Maddie quickly tallied what she knew of recent world events—precious little she now realized—and compared them with past events. The past had often seen severe natural disasters of the kind the Bible warned would mark the last days, but eventually, things always returned to normal. Could this be one of those times?

No, she shook her head. No, there was something decidedly different this time. Something felt malicious rather than accidental about what was going on. A shiver ran down her spine, and she realized she was still standing between the inner and outer doors of the prison foyer. She pushed open the outer door and burst out into the parking lot, feeling as though demons were pursuing her. It wasn't until the cold, fresh air hit her face that she realized she hadn't told Daniel about Lyn's pregnancy. This thought brought another on its heels. Suddenly, it was imperative that she locate her daughter immediately.

CHAPTER SIX

Maddie woke from a few hours of sleep in time to run a comb through her hair and dress quickly for her job at the diner. She hadn't been able to find Lyn before exhaustion overtook her and forced her to lie down. Though her sleep had been restless and short, she felt better when she woke up. However, a sense of urgency to find her daughter still filled her.

"God, You know where Lyn is. Please protect her. Keep her safe. Help me find her." She wolfed a dry toast and some weak tea before brushing her teeth and pulling on her coat. Grabbing up her keys and purse, she opened the apartment door to go out.

She had thought the apartment was chilly. When she stepped outside, she immediately understood why. It was cold—really, really cold. The kind of cold that usually came in January and forced people to stay indoors. She checked the thermometer and gasped. It was thirty degrees below zero. Unheard of in March.

Maddie knew she'd never be able to walk to the diner in this cold without more layers. She dashed back into the apartment and pulled three sweaters and an old pair of wind pants over her uniform. She had only one pair of knitted mittens, one hat, and a scarf, but she pulled these firmly on again and went back outside.

The cold was insidious. It stole beneath all her layers, chilling her to the bone. The walk to the diner was intolerable. Several times she was sure she couldn't go on. The wind drove the cold into her cheekbones, which were unprotected, and the pain was excruciating. She would have gladly broken her rule and hitched a ride, but there were no cars on the road. She half wondered if she was going to walk all the way to the diner, only to find it closed because no one could get their cars started.

Finally, Maddie arrived. She couldn't even feel the metal and glass of the door as she crashed against it and fell gratefully into the warm, bright interior of the diner. She knew without a doubt that if the place had been closed, she couldn't have walked all the way back to her apartment without freezing to death. She staggered to an empty booth and sat for a moment, letting the heat sink into her, grimacing as feeling returned to her cheeks, fingers, and toes.

"You didn't walk!" a woman's voice exclaimed. "You didn't! Why, you'd freeze solid!"

Maddie nodded. "I did. I had to. I have to save my gas allowance. Besides, my car would never start on a day like today."

"You shouldda called in sick then."

Debbie Barstow slipped into the seat across from Maddie and eyed her with concern. "You gonna be all right?"

"I'll be fine. I just need to thaw out a little."

Debbie's large eyes seemed even larger today and her face more pinched as she leaned across the table and dropped her voice. "My neighbors got took."

"Someone robbed them?"

"No," Debbie shook her head with impatience. "They got took. Somebody come and took 'em in the night. Like you read about in the papers."

"I don't read the papers. Who took them? Where?"

"They got took a'cause they're Christians. The Raynards been my neighbors for fifteen years, ever since they moved here from Tennessee. They lost their kids in a bad accident, and the grandma and grandpa too. Then they had some more kids—nice kids they was. Two girls and a little boy. He was only like this." She held up her hand, indicating the height of a toddler.

"Last night I hear cars drive up, two cars and a big truck. They was hard to miss a'cause my dogs barked at 'em. I looked out the window to see what they was barking at, and some men I didn't know was taking the Raynards out of their house. Them kids was crying, and they all looked scared. They put 'em in the truck and drove away.

"This morning I went over to see if they come back. They was still gone, and the worst of it was that the door was standing wide open. In this weather! That's when I knew they wasn't comin' back. They'd got took."

"But who would take them?"

"The government," Debbie supplied knowingly. "I read the papers every day a'cause Dickie gets one free working at the printing press. It's a independent paper, so it tells the truth. They been talkin' about all the Christians getting took all over. But mostly it's been in cities. They have these big raids, just like the Nazis used to, and round up all the Christians. Sometimes they raid a church service and take the whole church."

"Where do they take them?" Maddie fought to keep her teeth from chattering when she talked. She could feel her stomach clenching in fear. And although her body still shook involuntarily from the cold, she no longer noticed.

Debbie shrugged her narrow shoulders. "Some say they bring 'em to camps, like concentration camps. Some say they bring 'em to big pits and just shoot 'em. Some say they put 'em in jails and now the jails is stuffed to overflowing, with people dying right and left from disease. One thing for sure is that nobody has never seen 'em again."

If they are bringing them to jails, Maddie thought, *and the jails have stepped up executions of Christians, then it doesn't take a genius to figure out where they're ending up. But women and children too? It can't be possible.*

"My sister lives out near Burlington—that's kind of a big city, I guess—and she said she knows lots of people who been took. She said nobody talks about it a'cause they're scared of gettin' took too. You can't never tell who's gonna get took next. Mostly they take Christians though." Debbie twisted her long, bony fingers nervously. "I'm scared. What if I get took? Or worse, what if I don't get took? Does that mean I'm not really a Christian? Is it just the real Christians that get took, and the rest of us just think we're Christians but we're nothin' but big, fat fakes?"

"No," Maddie said immediately and confidently. She was rewarded by a look of relief in Debbie's eyes. "There's nothing in the Bible that says you'll know you're a Christian by whether you get taken in the end times. But I believe we are in those end times now." She was surprised to find how easily this assertion sprang to her lips and shocked to realize that it was no longer a question in her mind but a strong conviction in her heart. These *were* the end times—she'd never been more certain of anything.

"What does that mean?" Debbie looked every bit as frightened as she sounded.

Maddie knew Debbie hadn't been a Christian for long and had wrestled hard with some cherished sins in her life. Every now and then she fell down, but she always got back on her feet, dusted herself off, asked God for forgiveness, and went on. She was still a "baby" Christian, and Maddie didn't want to frighten her unnecessarily with information she didn't need to know. At the end of the day, it all boiled down to one thing anyway. God would take care of His children no matter what.

"Look," Maddie said, "the end of the world is coming. It's been coming for a long time, but now I think it's here. That's a good thing, right? It means we're going home to heaven to be with God."

"Yeah," Debbie said hesitantly. "But it's this part—what we're goin' through right now—that I'm worried about."

"You don't need to be," Maddie assured her. "God has promised never to leave or forsake us. He'll help us through whatever we have to go through. The important thing is to trust Him. If we do that, we can't go wrong."

"You're sure?"

"I'm sure. I'm going to tell you a Bible verse from Psalms, and you can repeat it to yourself whenever you're scared or worried or just need to know what God wants you to do. OK?"

"OK," Debbie said, and she leaned forward, her whole concentration on Maddie.

" 'Hear my cry, O God; attend to my prayer. From the end of the earth I will cry to You, when my heart is overwhelmed; lead me to the rock that is higher than I' " (Psalm 61:1, 2, NKJV).

" 'The rock that is higher than I,' " Debbie whispered. She smiled, and suddenly it seemed as though she was lit up from the inside. "Jesus is the Rock that's higher than I!"

"Yes," Maddie agreed. "Yes, He is. And He'll always be there for you, no matter what. So you don't have to worry. He'll be with you if you're taken or if you're not. He'll be with you no matter what happens to you."

"You two going to get any work done today, or you just going to sit there like a couple of paying customers and take up space?" a gruff voice groused mildly. Auggie Mock, the owner of the diner, peered out through the shelves from his position at the grill.

Maddie started. She hadn't known he was there. How much had he heard, and what had he thought of it? "Sorry, Auggie," she murmured.

She stood up and began removing her outer layers. She smoothed her hair and hung her winter clothes in her locker in a room beside the restrooms. Pulling an order pad out of her apron pocket, she scanned the diner booths, but they were all empty. She glanced at Auggie, but he was innocently wiping down a counter.

Had he only wanted them to stop talking? Or did he have a more sinister purpose in mind? Would she come to work tomorrow and find Debbie missing? Or would she wake up in the dead of night to a pounding on the door followed by a long ride in a cold truck to an unknown destination?

Maddie swallowed hard. The more she thought about what Debbie had said, the more worried she became. What if Lyn had been taken? What if that was why she hadn't come home?

"O God," Maddie prayed, "lead me to the Rock that is higher than I."

BOOK ONE:
THE BEGINNING OF THE END

CHAPTER SEVEN

By the time Maddie's shift ended, the temperature outside had reached ninety-five degrees. Thick, black clouds boiled ominously overhead, and thunder banged and echoed, while jagged forks of lightning split the heaving cloud masses. No rain fell, and the air was so thick with humidity that it was hard to breathe. Sometime after midnight, Auggie had nixed the heat and turned on the air-conditioner full blast.

Debbie offered to give Maddie a ride home so she wouldn't have to walk in the heat carrying all her winter clothes, and Maddie gratefully accepted. The first thing she saw when they pulled into the parking lot of her apartment building was Justin's smart red Porsche convertible. "Lyn's home!" she cried, nearly weeping with relief and joy.

Debbie leaned over to give her a quick hug before she got out, and Maddie hugged her back forcefully. "Remember 'the rock that is higher than I.' "

"I will," Debbie promised.

Maddie took the stairs two at a time and threw open the door to her apartment. "Lyn, I was so worried," she called out. Then the gladness died as she saw Justin sprawled on the couch and talking on his cell phone.

"Yeah, I'll call you back," he was saying. "Keep looking."

"Justin," Maddie faltered. "Where's Lyn?"

"That's what I'd like to know." He flicked the phone shut and shoved it into a pocket of his jeans. "Didn't she come back here?" He fixed her with a narrow gaze, his eyes cold and hard as marble.

"What do you mean 'come back here'? When did you see her last?"

"So she's not here. I was sure she'd come back. I figured she'd come crawling back to me after she'd had time to think it over."

"Think what over?"

"Not that it's any of your business, really, but the abortion. I want her to have an abortion. You do know she's pregnant, don't you? The last thing I need right now is a little brat running around and messing things up."

Maddie flinched as though he'd slapped her. "Not my business? Lyn is fifteen years old. She is a *child!* She's *my* child! I could have you brought up on charges, young man." As soon as the words were out of her mouth, Maddie knew she shouldn't have spoken them.

Justin rocketed off the couch. As he approached her, Maddie could smell the distinct odor of marijuana clinging to his clothes. He towered over her, and his look was menacing. "What did you say?" he demanded.

Maddie backed away slightly, but he pressed closer, invading her space, intimidating her. "I won't. I wouldn't. I just want what's best for Lyn. Can't you just leave her here with me? Just leave her, Justin."

"I can't leave her!" he roared, and Maddie felt her knees buckle in fear. "What do you think I'm doing here? If I could just let her go, I would. I love her. I want what's best for her too, you know. And it's not best for us to raise a child."

"Let me raise it," Maddie pleaded. "You won't have to do a thing."

"Sure, I can just see that," Justin sneered. "I can see you raising my kid to be a little church mouse. Over my dead body. You make me sick!"

"But you don't want the child. Why do you care?" He wasn't being reasonable, and for a second, Maddie forgot how afraid she was of him. All she could think about was the helpless child Lyn was carrying.

"No," he spat. "No, I don't want it. But you aren't getting it either. Just because I don't want to raise my own kid doesn't mean I want to abandon it to the likes of you either. That's no kind of life. I'd rather see it dead."

"You don't think—" Maddie began, a horrible thought occurring to her.

Justin understood immediately. "That she went and had it done?" he said, finishing her sentence.

"She wouldn't," Maddie whispered, hoping and praying she was right. Surely, Lyn wouldn't have been desperate enough to go through such a torturous experience alone. Surely, she would have come to Maddie first; surely, she would have given her a chance to talk her out of it, to reassure her that an abortion was the wrong thing to do.

"She would," Justin countered. "She would because I told her I'd never see her again if she didn't. But I didn't think she'd do it right away."

"She could be on some doctor's examining table right now." Maddie was so scared and sick thinking about it that she nearly threw up. "Or she could be dead somewhere of complications. You might have killed her! Get out! Get out of my house! I don't ever want to see you again!"

In her fury, Maddie didn't stop to think that Justin was bigger than she was. She didn't wonder what she would do if he resisted. She simply grabbed his arm, catching him off-balance, and threw all her weight against him, propelling him out the open door.

"And never come back!" she screamed, slamming the door. She sagged against it, sobbing. Through the thin wood, she heard him shrieking curses, and she felt the blows as he hammered on the door until his fury was spent. Then he clattered heavily down the staircase, and she heard him burn rubber as his car peeled out of the driveway.

Maddie slowly sank onto the floor, weeping. She felt as though she would certainly die there of a broken heart. Then it occurred to her that if Lyn was trying to get an abortion, she might not have succeeded yet. She was about to get up and search the yellow pages for the names of all the local clinics when a soft voice stopped her.

"Mom?"

At first, Maddie thought maybe she was hearing things. But then Lyn's form materialized from the darkness of the hallway.

"Mom?"

"Lyn!"

Maddie scrambled to her feet and threw herself at her daughter, laughing and crying. "Lyn! You're OK!"

For the first time in months, Lyn returned her hug—even seemed to be clinging to her.

"Yes, I'm OK. Everything is OK."

"The baby?"

"The baby is OK too." A thin smile touched Lyn's lips, but it wasn't a happy one. Lyn seemed to have aged years in the few short days she'd been gone. Her eyes were haggard holes in her face, and the skin around her mouth was pinched. She had an ashen complexion and looked brittle.

"Then you didn't . . ."

"No. I thought about it. I even went to a clinic and asked about it. But I couldn't do it. A baby is a baby—a human being. Maybe it shouldn't be here, but that's not the baby's fault, is it? I don't have the right to kill anyone, much less a baby I helped create." Here Lyn broke down.

Maddie comforted her daughter, making soothing sounds against her hair as she held her and rocked slightly back and forth. Relief and gratitude flooded through her, and she breathed a prayer of thanks. "It's OK. Everything will be OK now."

"It won't, it won't," Lyn wailed. "How can it be? My life is ruined. I'm fifteen! I can't have a baby. And it'll hurt." At this thought, she lifted her tear-stricken face to her mother. "It will, won't it?"

Maddie almost smiled. "Don't worry about that now," she said. "The important thing is that you're safe, the baby is safe, and we're together." She glanced at the door, remembering Justin. "How did you manage to elude Justin?" she asked.

Lyn wiped the tears from her face with the back of her hand. "I hid behind the false door in the closet, the one they used in the Underground Railroad."

The landlord had pointed out this feature of the apartment proudly. Maddie had been unimpressed at the time. It was historically interesting, but the space was worthless as far as storage was concerned. They had tried to store the Christmas ornaments in it the first year but had forgotten where they'd put them and did without. Lyn had discovered them the following July when playing hide-and-seek with Brian. At this moment, though, Maddie blessed the abolitionists who had built the hiding space, and she felt a new empathy for the slaves who had used it.

"Justin didn't look very hard anyway," Lyn was saying, "but he stayed for at least an hour. I thought my legs would go to sleep while I waited. It was cramped in there."

"You heard what he said."

It was more a reflection than a question, but Lyn answered anyway.

"Yeah. I don't believe him anymore, though. I mean, I believe him about not wanting the baby, but I don't believe that he loves me. I thought he did right up until I told him I was pregnant. But you should have seen his face, Mom. He got all ugly, and I thought he was going to hit me."

She pulled back the neck of her T-shirt to reveal angry red marks on her neck.

"He grabbed me and called me all kinds of bad names. He said he'd kill me and then we wouldn't have to worry about any of this. Then he told me I had to have an abortion no matter what I wanted. He said he didn't plan to marry me and his parents would never pay me for having his illegitimate child—as if I did this to make him marry me or to get money from his rich parents!"

Lyn's voice rose in indignation, and her face flushed with shame and embarrassment.

"It was an accident. It never should have happened—and it wouldn't have if I'd been following God the way I was brought up to do.

"You know," she said reflectively, "when I started dating Justin, I knew what would probably happen. But it was exciting to be liked by someone as cool and popular as Justin. And I really thought he did like me. The more I did for him, the more I thought he'd like me. But he was just using me. All that time, he was using me. Why couldn't I see it?" she asked bitterly.

"Why couldn't King David see it was wrong to take Bathsheba and kill Uriah? Why couldn't Judas see that betraying Jesus was wrong? Why did Saul persecute Christians? Sin makes us stupid, honey," Maddie said simply. "Sin makes us stupid."

"I've been stupid, all right." Lyn's voice was rueful, and she rubbed her belly as though it already bulged with the growth of her baby. "And now I'm going to pay for it. And so is this little one. But, Mom, what will we do?"

"The right thing," Maddie said firmly. "We'll do the right thing."

CHAPTER EIGHT

Maddie decided it would be safest for Lyn to go with her when she went to work at the nursing home. Lyn napped on the couch in the nurses' lounge while Maddie carried out her duties. After her shift, they spent the evening together cooking supper and stayed up most of the night talking about their future and making plans.

Lyn, who was afraid of Justin, thought they should get out of town and start over somewhere else with new identities. Maddie, who was also afraid of Justin, explained that they didn't have enough money to move anywhere. She would have no job, and what about Daniel? Who would visit him if they pulled up roots and left? In the end, they decided to lie low until they could talk with their pastor.

Maddie had a vague memory of hearing talk about the church family going into the mountains to avoid persecution. At the time, she'd been too absorbed with other problems in her life to give it much consideration, but now it seemed like the only solution. It would get them out of Justin's way, but not so far away that Maddie couldn't run to town for her visits with Daniel. She decided to broach the subject with him on her next visit.

The weather, which had alternated between record-breaking highs and lows, evened out in the seventies the day she went to visit Daniel. She wore a cotton skirt and blouse and made every effort to look nice for her visit. She checked in at the front desk as usual, but instead of buzzing her in, a guard she didn't recognize told her to take a seat and said the warden would be out to see her shortly.

Maddie settled herself on one of the uncomfortable metal chairs in the waiting area and felt her stomach clench in fear. She'd never been asked to wait before, and she wondered what was wrong. She deeply dreaded what the warden had to say to her and prayed that it had nothing to do with the executions of Christian prisoners. She'd seen Daniel only the week before; surely he hadn't been executed already!

"Mrs. Gray?" The warden was a short man, meticulously groomed and impeccably dressed. His face was set in serious lines; his eyes grave. The look he bore confirmed her worst suspicions. Daniel was dead.

"You've killed him, haven't you?" she heard herself say, her voice deadpan and disembodied.

The warden's mouth worked as though he might try to offer some excuse, some explanation, some platitudes to make her feel better, but then seemed to reconsider. "Daniel Gray was executed by lethal injection at six o'clock this morning," he said.

"This morning?" Maddie couldn't believe it. She had missed seeing Daniel again by a mere six hours. Why had no one warned her? Why had no one said how close the time was? Then she remembered Daniel's kiss, their first kiss since his incarceration, and she knew he had been trying to tell her. He'd been trying to prepare her for the worst. He'd known he might never see her again this side of heaven.

But they had a hope, she reminded herself. It didn't matter that Daniel wasn't here in the prison. In fact, Daniel had probably been relieved to leave the place where he'd been confined for so long. He would have known that the next thing he'd be conscious of was Jesus returning with His angels to free earth from Satan. He would have known that no matter how much time passed after his execution, the next instant of his awareness would bring the reuniting of his family. He'd be able to put his arms around his wife; there'd be no visiting room table between them, no locks on the door and bars on the windows. No one would be able to separate them again.

No, Maddie realized, Daniel might be gone, but this was not the end. It was only the beginning of the end. There were important things for her to attend to now, and she couldn't afford to waste time mourning for her beloved husband. She had a lot to do in order to prepare to meet him again. Most importantly, she had to take care of their daughter and her unborn child. That was her responsibility now.

"I'm sorry," the warden was saying, "world conditions are so unstable that we aren't allowed to divulge the execution schedule to anyone outside the prison system, so we couldn't notify you. I'm sorry for the inconvenience."

Inconvenience? Maddie almost laughed bitterly in his face. He was responsible for the termination of countless lives, and he thought it only inconvenient? She bit her tongue. Now was not the time to call authority into accountability. Instead, she nodded as though too choked up to speak. Avoiding the warden's eyes so her own wouldn't betray her, she turned on her heel and walked quickly out of the prison, determined to put as much distance as possible between herself and it.

There was no reason to save her gas allowance now, so on the way home she made a detour to her pastor's house. The small, white, ranch-style house looked deserted. The yard and gardens had grown leggy from neglect—flowers and bushes choked out by aggressive weeds. The bricks of the walkway were chipped and displaced. She edged along them gingerly to reach the front door, her heart sinking.

When she knocked, she could hear a tentative shuffling inside, and presently, the pastor cracked the door open and peered out. Through the opened door, she could see into the living room. In the darkened interior, she could just make out piles of boxes taped up and ready to be moved.

"Are you leaving for the woods or moving away?" she asked in alarm.

"Sister Gray, come in, come in." Pastor Mitchell was a soft-spoken, courteous, elderly man whose practiced manners reflected a bygone era. He shut the door behind her carefully. Heavy shades were drawn across the living-room windows, blocking the light and making the small space stuffy with recycled air.

Pastor Mitchell motioned to the boxes and the windows. "We want to maintain a low profile," he explained. "No need to advertise that we're leaving. You've heard, I suppose, about the raids?"

Maddie nodded. "I haven't seen any."

"Be grateful," he said, his old voice thin and wavering. "They took my neighbors two nights ago. I thought they would come for me next, but they didn't. I served as a medic in the second world war, you know. Brought back a lot of painful memories."

"I'm sorry." Maddie didn't know what else to say.

"Nothing for you to be sorry about, my dear. Now, what can I do for you?" He tipped his head to one side as he regarded her, a helpful expression on his face. He was a nice man, and Maddie wished he could have held Brian's funeral service—and Daniel's, if that had been possible. But their church had been shut down for almost a year now. The members met in people's homes on an ever-changing, secretive, rotating schedule. It reminded her of what she imagined the early Christians had to do.

"I want to come with you. To the woods, I mean. My daughter and I."

"By all means, by all means," Pastor Mitchell said quickly. "As you can see, we're leaving almost immediately. All of the men and some of the women and children are already living in a secluded area we found in the woods adjacent to Lake Memphramagog. They're in crude buildings to be sure, and they've suffered terribly with the sudden temperature changes, but God has provided. Our bread and water are sure. I leave tonight with the last of our members and some of their friends who want to join our number. You and Lyn are certainly welcome to join us. We thought you had already found shelter, my dear, or we would most assuredly have confirmed your plans before we left. I apologize most sincerely."

"It's OK, Pastor Mitchell. I haven't been able to make the meetings lately. A lot has been happening. Maybe you heard about Brian . . ."

"Yes, most sad. We were in the woods at the time, making preparations. But we heard on one of our trips back for supplies. I'm so very sorry, my dear."

"And today I found out that Daniel . . ."

Maddie couldn't bring herself to say it, but Pastor Mitchell was ahead of her, and his eyes flooded with tears. " 'Man is born to trouble as surely as sparks fly upward,' " he quoted. "How you have suffered! Poor child."

Maddie shook her head wretchedly. "That's not all. Lyn, my daughter, is pregnant and in danger from the father of her child. He wants her to have an abortion. That's why we need to come with you to the woods. If it weren't for Lyn, I guess I wouldn't care what happened to me anymore."

"God cares what happens to you," Pastor Mitchell said firmly, "so you must care what happens to you. You are His temple, child; His residence here on earth. He loves us with so powerful a love that we cannot even comprehend it. You have taken care of your earthly responsibilities. Now it is time to take care of your heavenly ones. Come, pray with me."

Maddie knelt stiffly on the worn living-room carpet and allowed Pastor Mitchell to take her hands in his own. The skin of his palms was so papery thin that she wondered why it didn't rip.

THE THIRD COMING

"Our holy heavenly Father," Pastor Mitchell began. His soft voice lifted with a happy quality as though he were meeting a precious friend again. It was easy to see that Jesus and His Father were more than names in an inspired book to the pastor—they were intimate acquaintances.

"Father, we know that our time here is short. We look forward with great longing to Your soon return. Oh, come Lord Jesus; come quickly. Come and save Your people, who long to see You.

"I bring to You my friend Madeline, who needs the comfort of Your love. She has lost those most dear to her. You understand her suffering because You also lost Someone dear to You. Comfort her in her hour of grief. Hold her firmly in Your right hand, and keep her safe from the evil one, whose wrath threatens us all.

"And as Your Son was restored to You, restore Madeline's family to her. Bring her safely into Your presence in the company of her husband, her son, and her daughter. We know You do not want to lose even one of these precious souls. We ask You to watch over the remainder of this little flock. Be with Madeline as she prepares to join us in the safe haven You have prepared for us. Guide her and Lyn to safety. Be with Lyn also, and reconcile her to Yourself. Thank You for being a God of second chances.

"We ask for all these kindnesses knowing that You want what is best for us. Since we can see only dimly, as in a mirror, we place ourselves in Your will, knowing that You see clearly and are merciful and good and that Your kindness will never end. We trust Your faithfulness to us and believe in Your love for us. Forgive us, I pray, if we have failed You in any way. Bring us to a knowledge of our sin so that we might confess it. Do not let anything, small or great, interfere with our relationship with You. I pray and ask all these things in the name of Your Son, Jesus, through whom we are saved and by whose mercy we will share eternal life. Amen."

"Amen," Maddie said. She faltered slightly as she stood, wiping tears from her eyes. "That was a beautiful prayer," she said, fishing for a tissue to blow her nose.

"Our words don't do His love justice," Pastor Mitchell said smiling, "but I know the Holy Spirit will intercede and tell Him my true feelings on the matter. As for you, my dear, where shall we meet you and Lyn?"

"We can come here." Maddie said. Then she paused briefly to calculate how long it would take Lyn and her to pack. "I have a little money set aside, and there's the car and a few other things we have that we could sell—"

Pastor Mitchell stopped her. "If you have any cash, bring it. Leave your other valuables. Don't try to sell anything; it might make people suspicious. Come with the least amount of possessions you can. Bring any food you have in the house. We leave the rest to God. He has promised that bread shall be given us, and our water shall be sure."

"We'll meet you here tonight," Maddie promised.

"We leave at midnight. Be sure to come before then. If something happens, we will try to find you, if you will stay where you are. May God keep you, child."

Pastor Mitchell wrung her hand gently and escorted her to the door. Maddie's head whirled with activity. There was so much to do. First, she must stop by Jean's to collect Lyn, who was hiding there. Then they must pack and get everything ready to go. Tonight they would be safe at last.

CHAPTER NINE

Maddie was absorbed in thought at a four-way stop when she felt the first rumble. At first, she assumed the old car was shuddering. But as the vibration grew stronger, she realized something worse was causing it. She didn't know if it was safer to stay in the car or to get out, but she felt as though the interior of the car were closing in on her. In a panic, she flung the door open and scrambled out of the car. The power of the earthquake immediately threw her to the ground.

Maddie watched helplessly as her car was bounced around like the toy of an angry child. Both a rumbling sound and a great ripping noise filled the air as buildings, pavement, and earth were torn open. The earthquake seemed to go on forever. Not a hundred yards away, a barn was swallowed by the earth as if a giant monster had yawned beneath it. Maddie closed her eyes and clung to the ground, convinced that the end had come at last. She prayed for God to save her and to save Lyn.

The earthquake stopped as abruptly as it had started. Maddie cautiously opened her eyes and looked heavenward, convinced that she would see Jesus with a host of angels, but the sky was empty of anything except some boiling clouds. She got shakily to her feet and looked for her car. It rested in a cornfield ten feet from the road. Her legs wobbling, Maddie made her way over to it. One of the windows was cracked, but otherwise it seemed unharmed. Tentatively, she pulled open the door and slid behind the wheel. The door squealed in protest and resisted, but she was able to shut it behind her. The engine started easily, and she drove over the lumpy ground back onto the road.

Maddie drove slowly, wary lest parts of the road might be missing or impassable. Nothing but devastation met her eye for miles. Barns and houses had splintered into matchsticks, trees had been pulled up by the roots, and chunks of pavement from the road rested in newly created ditches. Maddie had to skirt several bad sections, but she continued to find a route to travel that was largely unharmed.

When she hit the outskirts of town, she found the traffic piled up in a mass of confusion. Cars and trucks vied to pass each other in bizarre ways, taking no notice whatsoever of the traffic signs or rules of the road. An eighteen-wheeler passed Maddie on the right, the driver blowing his horn and bearing down on her so closely that she was sure he'd roll right over the top of her car. He took off her side-view mirror and pelted on, oblivious to the congested traffic ahead of him.

Maddie eased her car off to a side street and took the back route to Jean's house, where she knew she would find Lyn waiting for her. She wouldn't tell Lyn about Daniel unless Lyn asked her outright. It would be better to wait until they reached the haven of the woods, where they could grieve in relative safety and peace.

It seemed that no house had been left unscathed. Most had shattered windows or doors that hung lopsided from one hinge. As she passed her own apartment building, she craned to see how badly it had been damaged. The end of the building farthest from her apartment had collapsed, but her own apartment seemed to have come through mostly intact. She hoped Jean's house had fared as well.

Maddie pressed up as close as she could to the windshield as she approached the house. It was still standing, though the picket fence was a shambles—broken up like popsicle sticks scattered on the lawn. The roof had lost some shingles, but otherwise the house appeared unharmed. She pulled the car into the driveway, now a mass of chopped up asphalt, and got out carefully.

A hand whisked the curtain back and then dropped it as Jean opened the door and motioned her in anxiously. Her dark eyes roamed the streets until she was satisfied, and then she closed the door and turned to Maddie. "You've got to get out of here now," she hissed. "It isn't safe. That boy will see your car, and he'll know she's here. He's been up and down the road every couple of hours. I think he suspects she might be here. I've been frightened out of my mind!"

Maddie was alarmed but determined not to show it. "Is Lyn OK?" she asked.

"Yes, she's fine. After the earthquake, I told her to go lie down. It shook us up pretty bad, let me tell you. But the old place held together, thankfully. On the news they're saying it was simply off the Richter scale, and we're not anywhere near ground zero. Some of my china came right off the shelves and made quite a mess, but we got that picked up. How was Daniel?"

Maddie shook her head and tried to control herself.

Jean's lips pursed angrily. "I should have known. You poor thing. And no warning. It's unconstitutional, that's what." She patted Maddie awkwardly on the shoulder. "It's that warden's fault. He's the most crooked man I know. Wesley James. I went to school with that no-good scoundrel. I can tell you his character was seriously lacking then; I can only imagine what kind of a reprobate he's become. Power, you know, goes straight to a person's head. I'll tell you what, I'm going to start a citizen's coalition and get him ousted. Maddie, you must write a report about this, and we'll bring it to the authorities."

Maddie felt her chin drop. "Jean, there's no time for any of that. None of it matters. This is the end."

"The end?" Jean's brow furrowed in puzzlement. "The end of what? Maddie, that man will keep disobeying the law and abusing his authority until someone steps in and says enough is enough."

"You don't understand. It doesn't matter anymore. The warden is finished no matter what. The end of the world is coming right now. Lyn and I are going away with our church family to a safe place. Come with us. You'll be safe there, and we can wait for Jesus to come."

"Madeline Gray, are you out of your mind?" Jean stepped back as though she'd been struck. "I know this news is devastating, and coming on top of everything else that's been happening lately, I can see why you might come unglued. But be reasonable. Things are bad, surely, but it's not the end of the world. There's no need to become flakey just because of a streak of bad luck."

Maddie stared at Jean as though seeing a mirage. Something was very wrong here. Either Jean, who watched the news on television and was infinitely better informed than she was herself, had talked herself into believing that life would go on as it always had, or she was doing an awfully good job of acting like that's what she believed. Maddie searched Jean's face, but her friend seemed sincere.

"You know, they've been taking Christians," Maddie ventured. "They just show up at your house in the middle of the night and take you away.

Even if you don't believe the end of the world is coming, Jean, you and Ernie should come with us. Aren't you afraid you'll be next? You're a Christian."

"Of course I'm a Christian," Jean snapped. "And no, I'm not worried. Come here."

Jean strode purposefully down the hall, and Maddie reluctantly followed her into her pretty bedroom, all done up in a country style with yellows and blues and flowers everywhere, like a field. Jean opened the door of a nightstand, exposing a small safe inside. Her fingers expertly whirled a knob until Maddie heard a soft click and the door swung open. Inside, piles of gold coins covered the safe's shelf. Maddie thought it looked like a pirate's treasure. It was unexpected and overwhelming.

"See this?" Jean swept her hand toward the safe proudly. "If anyone dares show up at our door in the middle of the night to demand we leave, don't you think the sight of this stack of gold will change their minds?"

"What if they take it and you with it?" Maddie squeaked, still overwhelmed by the sight of so much money in one place.

"This is only the tip of the iceberg," Jean snorted. "There's plenty more where this came from. But only Ernie and I know where it is. We have enough stashed away to weather any storm. When this all blows over—and it will all blow over eventually, mark my words—we'll be in good shape."

"Where did you get so much money?"

"We worked for it," Jean said, her voice flinty. Maddie knew better than to ask any more questions along that line. She didn't know what else to say.

"Mom?" Lyn stood sleepily in the door of the bedroom. "Are we leaving now?"

"Lyn!" Maddie said with relief. She ushered Lyn down the hallway as Jean turned back to lock the safe. "Yes, get your things. Jean says she's seen Justin driving by the house, so we need to get out now."

"Where are we going?"

"Home. We'll pack there and then meet the church folks at Pastor Mitchell's house. We're going with them tonight. Then we'll be safe."

"All set?" Jean asked brightly as she rejoined them in the living room.

THE THIRD COMING

"Yes, we're all set. Thank you so much, Jean, for letting Lyn stay here while I was away," Maddie said. Her cheerfulness sounded forced in her own ears, but Jean didn't seem to notice. Maddie hugged her friend fiercely, wishing there was something she could say to convince her that she and Ernie should come with them. "Goodbye, Jean. God bless you."

"You too," Jean said, hugging her back. "I'll see you soon. Don't stay in the mountains forever."

Lyn returned with her bag, and they made their way to the car and drove quickly away. In her rearview mirror, Maddie could see Justin's Porsche turn onto Jean's street just as she pulled onto the main road. It would take some fancy driving to get home without Justin on their tail. She punched the gas and held on to the steering wheel, her knuckles white and a prayer in her teeth.

CHAPTER TEN

"The angels must be surrounding this car," Maddie said as she pulled into the parking lot of a bank a few blocks behind their apartment building. "Somehow we lost Justin. We'll have to park the car here in case he comes to look for us at the apartment."

They cut across several lots until they were close to the apartment. Then they looked around for a long time before deciding it was safe to make a dash across the parking lot to the stairs. Maddie was thankful that darkness had finally fallen. Only the faint wash of light from the few streetlights that still worked illuminated the small space.

Once inside, they bolted the door and pulled every curtain. "Pastor Mitchell said we should take only what we absolutely need," Maddie said. "Why don't you go pack? We'll leave as soon as we're done. It's getting late, and I'm so afraid they'll go without us. We're cutting it too close."

Maddie packed methodically. There wasn't much in her dresser drawers, so packing wasn't a complicated operation. She threw in a few of her favorite sweaters in case the weather turned cold again, some slacks, and some jumpers. Most of her other clothes were for work, and she left those in the drawers. She was just throwing in her toothpaste and toothbrush when she heard a pounding at the door.

Lyn appeared, wild-eyed, in Maddie's bedroom doorway and motioned for Maddie to follow her. Wordlessly, she complied. Lyn went straight to the secret panel in the closet of the back bedroom. Before she opened the panel, she pried up the bedroom window as silently as she could, then they crowded into the hiding place and slid the panel shut behind them.

The space was too small for two people. Their bodies were crammed so tightly together that Maddie could feel the beat of her daughter's heart. The air was close, and it already felt stale. She tried not to breathe. In her own ears, her breathing sounded like the heavy puffing of a locomotive. Surely, anyone prowling around looking for them would hear it.

Maddie had often wondered how escaping slaves felt as they fled for their lives and their freedom to the north. The stories in books seemed so romantic that you didn't really feel for their peril—not in the way you did when you were in their place, she thought wryly. She had certainly never considered the physical duress they suffered in their hiding places.

She could hear people moving through the house. When a man finally spoke, it sounded as though he were in the closet with them, and Maddie had to stifle a gasp.

"They were here, all right," the voice said. "Looks like we interrupted them too, because this suitcase isn't completely packed. Where do you suppose they were going in such a hurry?"

"There's no way out," another voice said, and Lyn squirmed next to Maddie. The voice was Justin's. "Look, they couldn't have jumped out of a window. This is the second story."

"I think they could have. The window is open . . ." They heard the scraping and squeak of the window as someone lowered it and then the man's voice again. "It'd be a mighty long fall, but you could survive a fall like that from here. If you were desperate enough, you might take the chance. How desperate do you think they were?"

"Desperate," Justin admitted. "At least the girl is."

"Do you think they knew we were coming?"

"They saw me following them, so they would have known I'd be coming. But there's no reason they should have expected you boys."

"And you're sure they're Christians?" The other voice sounded sterner. "You didn't set us up for your own personal vendetta, did you, son? You know there are heavy penalties for using the authorities to do your dirty work for you. If you've got a gripe with this girl, that's one thing; but if she and her mother are Christians, that's a whole other story."

"They're Christians, I swear!" Justin sounded angry and defiant. "I'll prove it to you." The men moved to another room, and Maddie heard them rummaging around and then a triumphant, "Ha! What did I tell you? A Bible, and look how much writing there is in it."

Oh, God, please don't let them take my Bible, Maddie prayed. She had placed it in the bottom of her suitcase when she started packing. Daniel had given the Bible to her when they got married, and it was the only one she had. It hadn't meant anything to him at the time; but later, after he'd become a Christian, he'd written her a special love note in the end pages. The Bible itself could be replaced, but its meaning to her could not.

"So it is," the man said thoughtfully. "Well, son, looks like you caught yourself some Christians, sure enough. The problem is, they've flown the coop for now. I think we'll have to come back another time. Meanwhile, we can take this into evidence. We'll need it sooner or later is my guess."

It sounded to Maddie as though the men moved off down the hall and left the apartment, but she couldn't be sure. The safest thing to do was to wait for a while. Lyn nudged her, and she spoke one soft word: "Wait."

The darkness was so complete in the closet and the air so thin that soon Maddie fancied she saw spots whirling in front of her eyes. Time passed, but it was impossible to tell how long. She felt Lyn slump against her; she hoped that only meant Lyn had fallen asleep. Sleep and remaining undetected were their only mercies.

Just before she succumbed to sleep herself, the spots before her eyes seemed to change to planets. They careened through the darkness of the solar system. One seemed bluer than the others, and a bright light blanketed it. As Maddie watched, the light lifted from the planet and it became dark. Then Maddie drifted into oblivion.

When she woke, the hiding place was relatively light; she could make out the grain of the wood. There was no sound from the apartment. After waiting what she judged to be maybe an hour, Maddie slowly opened the door, and she and Lyn fell out into the closet beyond. They couldn't move quietly because they had lost most of the feeling in their limbs. Maddie just prayed that the men had left no guards.

Her heart pounding in fear, Maddie motioned Lyn to stay in the closet while she checked things out. "God, make me strong," she prayed. "Go with me." Slowly, she placed one foot in front of the other and worked her way through the apartment. She found no one.

When she reached the living room, she noticed that the intruders hadn't bolted the door behind them. She didn't bolt it either. She thought that until she and Lyn figured out what to do, they'd best leave everything as the men had. She lifted the edge of the curtain slightly, and her heart dropped into her feet when she saw an unfamiliar car in the parking lot.

THE THIRD COMING

Someone had been left to watch the house. How long would the watcher remain out there? She and Lyn were trapped until he left. They were prisoners in their own home as surely as Daniel had been in the jail.

Soberly, she gathered some food and used the bathroom before returning to the bedroom. She told Lyn what she'd found, and together they ate in silence, each contemplating their fate and praying for guidance and deliverance.

"It would be best if we stayed in the hiding space for now," Maddie said finally. "It's the only safe thing to do. They could come back and check at any time. In a few days, they'll get sick of watching and they'll leave. Then it will be safe for us to go."

"Go where?" Lyn asked. "The church people have gone already. Do you know where they went?"

"No, honey, but God does," Maddie said. She felt a deep peace about this. God wouldn't forsake them. He would help them to safety in His own time.

"Do you think they'll go away?" Lyn asked. Her voice wavered and was laced with exhaustion. Dark half circles colored the sunken spaces beneath her eyes. Maddie was concerned for her. Staying in that small space was hard enough for Maddie—what must it be for Lyn, who was pregnant? She suddenly realized that she didn't even know how far along her daughter's pregnancy was.

"I think that they'll go away if God wants them to," Maddie answered simply. "Beyond that, I don't know. I don't like to think that God wants us to be taken, but I know that if He does, there's a reason for it. He'll make something good come from it, even if that good is only that we learn to trust Him implicitly. And I know that no matter what happens—whether we stay in the hiding space and eventually escape or they find us and take us away—God will be with us. There is no place on earth He wouldn't go with us and no place that people have found or created where they can hide us from Him. I don't know what sinful human beings will do—I can't even guess. But I know my God, and I know what He'll do."

Hugging her daughter, Maddie continued. "If I could take all this suffering from you onto myself, I would do it."

"I know, Mom." Lyn smiled wanly. "It'll be OK. God's in control."

BOOK ONE:
THE BEGINNING OF THE END

CHAPTER ELEVEN

For the next few days, Maddie and Lyn lived in the hiding space, coming out only when their limbs fell asleep. They would walk around until the circulation returned, eat something, and take care of their personal needs. Maddie checked the parking lot each time, but the car remained. It looked like there were two men inside.

"I'm tired," Lyn whimpered when they came out of the closet for some air on their third day in captivity. "And my stomach is upset. I can't eat any more cold canned beans; I feel like I'm going to throw up."

Maddie put her arm around her daughter. "I'm sorry, honey. I wish there was something I could do to help. We could try cooking something, but if they smell it, they'll find us. Do you want to take the risk?"

Lyn shook her head with resignation. "No. I just won't eat anything for a while. We don't have any crackers, do we?"

A search of the cupboards turned up one lone packet of rather ancient snack crackers that Lyn gratefully savored. "I never thought I'd be so thankful for stale crackers," she observed. When she was finished, she carefully wrapped up the remainder of the crackers and took them into the hiding space.

They decided to sleep on the floor just outside the closet that night. They'd take turns watching, and they'd get back in the closet at the slightest noise.

Maddie had the first watch. Lyn curled up near her and immediately fell into a deep sleep. Maddie felt herself begin to doze several times, but she shook herself awake. It was vital that she stay awake she told herself firmly. But the mental weariness of constantly staying on guard and the physical exhaustion worked together to dull her senses.

That's when she heard the voices. They were so loud that she thought they'd been discovered. But no one was in the darkened room.

She shook Lyn violently, and together they scrambled into the hiding place. As she stood with her knees trembling and her heart pounding, she realized that the voices were in the next apartment. The family who lived there were being taken. Maddie was dismayed to realize that she didn't even know those neighbors and hadn't realized they were Christians. Now her heart bled for them as children screamed and men shouted with harsh voices. She heard quiet sobs mixed with the thumping and crashes involved in their rapid packing.

In minutes, it seemed, it was over, and the apartment was silent. Maddie didn't dare risk getting out of the hiding place now. She resigned herself to another interminable night of discomfort. "At least," she said to herself, "we're here, and we're together." She floated in and out of consciousness until morning.

When she looked out at the parking lot on the fourth day, the car was gone. Dusk was approaching, and the street lamps were beginning to light up. "Quick," she told Lyn, "get your things. We're getting out of here."

"But where are we going?" Lyn protested. "We don't know where anyone is. Shouldn't we stay here at least until we figure out where to go?"

"What if they come back?" Maddie countered. "They know we'd return to the apartment eventually. I don't think it will ever be safe for us here. I think we should take a chance on getting out now. I believe God will show us where to go. We'll just follow where He leads."

Neither heard the front door open quietly while they were talking. And the footsteps of the intruder fell so softly that they didn't even realize someone had entered the house until he suddenly loomed in the doorway.

Maddie was the first to see him, and she felt her spirit sink. They'd been caught. All their careful hiding had been in vain.

For a moment or two, the three of them simply stared at each other. Then it began to cross Maddie's mind that this man wasn't behaving like the men who'd been pursuing them. He was young, maybe in his early twenties, and he was alone. Maybe they could overpower him.

"Are you Maddie Gray?" he asked softly at last.

Maddie nodded, not trusting her voice.

"I'm Thomas. Pastor Mitchell sent me. When you didn't arrive on time, he sent me and another man, Michael, to find out what happened. We saw you and your daughter enter the apartment, but before we could reach you, some men broke in. When you didn't come out with them and they posted someone to watch the apartment, we assumed that God was somehow hiding you from them. So we waited.

"A few hours ago, the men drove away. We thought it might be a ruse, so we continued to wait. But now we think it's time for you both to get out. Are you packed?"

"Yes," Maddie said, her voice breaking. "Yes, we're almost finished packing. Thank you so much for coming to get us. We didn't know where to go."

Thomas swayed slightly and reached for the doorjamb to catch himself. "I'm sorry. I'm a little light-headed. Michael and I didn't bring any food with us because we didn't intend to stay."

"You mean you haven't eaten in four days?" Maddie exclaimed softly. "You must eat something. We have a little food. Where is your friend?"

"Michael is outside. He'll warn us if anyone approaches the apartment. There's no time to eat right now. Bring whatever you have. We'll eat on the way." Maddie and Lyn hurriedly finished their packing while Thomas went to the kitchen to pack the edibles he deemed worthwhile.

As Maddie followed Lyn through the darkened apartment, lit only by the light from the street lamps, she looked around absently. She would never see this place again. *And good riddance,* she thought. She, Brian, and Lyn had done a lot of living in this awful place, but she thought of none of it now that it was time to leave. She wouldn't miss this dreary abode; she'd leave it without a backward glance. What filled her mind instead was all the living they were yet to do—with Daniel as well—in heaven and the new earth. Rather than being oppressed by earth's darkness, their lives would be lit by the glory of Jesus.

"Are you ready?" Thomas's voice broke into her thoughts. "Then let's go; there's no time to lose."

He led them down the rickety stairs to the parking lot, which they skirted to avoid the illumination of the streetlights. Michael was waiting in the shadows on the perimeter of the lot, and he nodded silently to them and took the bags from Lyn's hands. He was considerably older than Thomas, and the grooves worn into his weathered face cast dark shadows that crisscrossed his countenance.

The little group went on, dodging down alleys that smelled of cat urine and around the backsides of buildings whose ill-tended lots were pockmarked with broken bottles and debris. Maddie drank in deep draughts of the humidity-soaked air. It felt like years since she had breathed fresh air. A new storm was brewing, and the air seemed alive with electricity. Though no rain fell, heat lightning lit up the sky and helped her see where to place her feet.

She had just begun to tire when they ducked behind a hedge. Thomas and Michael had hidden their car on the side sheltered from the road. It was a small, old vehicle, but the four of them managed to squeeze in amidst the baggage. Thomas drove, and even in the relative safety of the car, he didn't speak. She could tell he was tense because his shoulders were tight and his knuckles white as he gripped the steering wheel, and beads of sweat stood out on his forehead.

Maddie passed him an apple, but he set it in his lap and continued to drive. Not until they were beyond the limits of the town and passing through mile after mile of farmland did he finally allow himself to relax enough to eat the apple. Michael was eating too, crushed into the backseat with Lyn and some extra luggage as well as what Maddie and Lyn had brought.

"Can I ask you a question now?" Maddie ventured.

Thomas nodded but continued to eat the apple—core, seeds, and all. The only thing that remained in his hand when he was finished was the stem. He tossed it out the window.

"What is it like, this place where you're taking us?"

"It's not the Ritz," Thomas said grimly. "Conditions are very primitive."

"How long do you think we'll have to stay there?"

He glanced sideways at her. "Well, it's hard to tell. Most everyone thinks this is the end, though some who are with us think this is just a testing time and that eventually we'll all have to go back to our homes."

"What do you think?"

He was silent for a moment, contemplating. Then he said, "I think it will be over soon—whether 'soon' is this week or next or a month or even six months."

Maddie nodded, satisfied. "I don't think it will be long either." She sighed. "Things seem to be happening so fast."

"We have a radio at the shelter so we can get news reports. Someone monitors it constantly. At the end of each shift, the listener gives a general report, and if anything significant has happened, we hold a meeting."

"How long have you been at the shelter?" Maddie asked.

"I've been living there for three months now. I was with the original team who went out to build it and make things ready." The pride in his voice was hard to miss. "I'm a construction worker by trade, so I was a natural choice. There were twelve of us, all men, living in tents while we built the shelters. We had studied books so we could build the structures to blend into the terrain. We're very hard to spot unless you know where to look. I don't kid myself though; if God's angels didn't hide us, we'd have been discovered already despite all the precautions we've taken."

"What kind of precautions?"

"The usual. The shelters don't have windows, and we don't allow lights in aboveground dwellings after sunset. We use gas to do the little bit of cooking and heating we need so there's no smoke to give us away. There's a curfew and noise ordinances, of course."

" 'Curfew' and 'ordinances'?" Maddie's mouth pulled down in a line of concern. "That all sounds so official."

Thomas's face was sober. "It *is* official. The lives of many people are at stake."

"How many people live there?"

"There are one hundred thirty-five at the moment."

Maddie tried to imagine that many people living in primitive conditions. Bathing, cooking, co-existing in a cramped space under constant restriction—it all seemed impossible.

"Surely, you didn't store enough food to feed that many people day after day?"

Thomas shook his head slowly, a look of wonderment on his face. "No, you're right. We thought at first that we could. But with the logistics . . . well, it was impossible. The same with the gas—we couldn't store enough. All the same, neither the food nor the gas has run out."

As Maddie was digesting this information, Thomas pulled off the side road on which they'd been bouncing from rut to rut for miles and turned onto an even bumpier cow path through the woods. The severe jostling prevented conversation; it was all Maddie could do to hang on as everything in the car's interior rattled, shifted, and bounced around.

Mercifully, after a short interval, Thomas brought the car to a stop and announced, "We're here." Maddie looked out through the dirty windows at her surroundings. It took her a few minutes to make out any sign of civilization, and when she did, she was amazed at how well camouflaged it all was.

She stepped from the car on wobbly legs and turned to help Lyn extricate herself from the backseat, wincing at the various lumps and bumps she'd sustained on their wild ride. Thomas and Michael were already dragging over large brush cuttings with which to cover the car. Maddie grabbed their luggage and piled it next to Lyn, who was watching the proceedings and looking around with great interest.

When Thomas and Michael had hidden the car completely so that no one on the ground or in the air could spot it, they grabbed armfuls of luggage and led the way to a long, low cabin—the first one Maddie had spotted when they arrived. "This is the community center," Thomas explained. "We'll get you situated later, but first we need to let Pastor Mitchell know you're here."

Almost before he stopped speaking, the door flew open and the elderly pastor shuffled out to greet them. "Madeline, Lyndell, we have prayed for your safety constantly. Thomas, Michael, faithful boys, come in, come in. There is stew on the burner, and Sarah has made some fresh bread." He gripped Maddie's hand warmly and smiled at her. "Welcome to the Lord's sanctuary for His followers."

Maddie stepped across the threshold into the darkened interior of the cabin. She felt as though she was a ship finally berthing in a safe harbor. Tension fled her body, and a deep weariness flooded her. She thought she could sleep for weeks.

BOOK ONE:
THE BEGINNING OF THE END

CHAPTER TWELVE

The weeks in the cabins flew by so fast that Maddie couldn't begin to number them. She had no idea how long she and Lyn had lived with the community of believers hiding in the woods. Rather than resenting the sequestration, Maddie found it to be one of the happiest experiences in her life.

The community had a common kitchen, and she had been assigned kitchen duties on a rotating shift. The meals were plain and plentiful. No one went hungry; the pot was full until the last bowl had been drawn from it and everyone was satisfied. The first time she witnessed this miracle, Maddie cried.

Other miracles followed so closely that she began to take them for granted. On her first morning, she helped to make the oatmeal. Annette, an older woman who was in charge of the kitchen, sent her to bring in the oats. Maddie had taken the bucket and made her way out a narrow, covered walkway to the shed where the supplies were kept. Big wooden barrels lined the back wall.

Maddie remembered lifting the lid of the oatmeal barrel and looking inside with dismay. There was just enough to fill her bucket, no more and no less. She had scraped the bottom of the barrel to get the last little bit out. When she was satisfied that she had scooped up all she could, she returned to the kitchen.

"There's no more oatmeal," she told Annette.

"No more?" Annette had answered, her voice thick with a Canadian accent. Then she had smiled and said, "I doubt that, but we'll see, eh? The good Lord will provide."

That's when Maddie remembered what Thomas told her about the food not running out. Sure enough, the next morning when she returned with the same bucket for the oats, the barrel held exactly the same amount as it had the day before. And when the oatmeal was cooked, the pot seemed bottomless until the last person had eaten and was full.

THE THIRD COMING

The same thing happened with all the other food—and the water. While the skies had threatened rain, they hadn't delivered, and the rain barrels should have been empty. But whenever anyone went to fill the water buckets, they always held just enough water for their needs.

In Maddie's first days there, someone had given her a Bible. Although she still keenly missed her own, she began to develop a fondness for the new one. It was a different translation than the one she was accustomed to, and she wondered if that accounted for the life it seemed to have. It seemed new each time she opened it. Texts she had memorized had new meanings for her when she read them in the unfamiliar wording. She found that she understood more and questioned less.

Maddie had asked Thomas about what she was experiencing with the Bible. "I don't know," he'd replied. "It may be the translation, but I think it has more to do with this time and our willingness to listen to what God has to say. Maybe it's the lack of distraction. You aren't the only person who has mentioned that effect though."

By far Maddie's favorite times were the Bible studies. These were held every evening in the common room, which was just barely large enough to accommodate everyone if they were willing to pack into it like sardines. And they were. Not a word of complaint was heard—not even when the air got stuffy and toes were trod upon or ribs were elbowed.

The members of the community were never idle because there was always something to cook or mend or study or write or discuss. Often, when a lull occurred in the activity, several people would find themselves in a discussion that drew others in.

Maddie was helping Lyn with a pile of mending one afternoon when they overheard an interesting conversation Thomas was having with a small group of believers about the judgment. "What if I'm not good enough?" a woman was asking. Maddie recognized her. She was a very nervous elderly woman who carried a small fluffy cat with her everywhere she went. She had asked Maddie to call her "Tildy."

"Good enough for what?" Thomas replied, his Bible open and on his knee.

"Good enough for Jesus to save me. You're saying that there's a judgment going on right now—"

"That's right," Thomas said. "The pre-Advent judgment. We know that Jesus began His work of judgment in the heavenly sanctuary in 1844, and—"

"So, how do I know He hasn't crossed me off His list?" Tildy asked. "I mean, what if I was thinking bad thoughts about my neighbor when He got to my name? Does that mean I'm lost even though I'm sitting here waiting for Him to come back and take me home? How can I know for certain if I'm going to be saved?" The old woman's voice cracked with the weight of emotion she felt.

Suddenly, Lyn was on her feet and pressing into the little group. Maddie half rose to go with her but decided against it and sank back into her seat. While Maddie had relaxed since their arrival, Lyn had become increasingly tense. Maddie sensed that her struggle was about to be resolved, so she said nothing. Instead, she continued sewing while listening to every word.

"How can we know we'll make it through the judgment?" Lyn asked, her voice high and tense. "What if we've messed up and ruined our lives? What if for a while we didn't live the way we knew we were supposed to? What if God judged us then, but we've repented now? How can we be sure?"

Thomas looked from one agonized face to the other, and Maddie prayed that he would find the words to calm the fears raging through Tildy and Lyn—and who knew how many of the others who were looking on but hadn't contributed to the conversation.

"God doesn't decide whether to accept or reject us during the judgment," he explained gently. "He doesn't pounce on us during a weak time and then cross our names off the list. He loves each of us more than we'll ever fathom. He doesn't want to lose a single one of us. Christ died for us—for all of us—not when we were good enough to save, but when we were still sinning. Let me read you something."

Thomas picked the Bible up from his lap and thumbed through the worn pages. "Here it is—in Matthew," he said and began to read. " 'Jesus spoke to them again in parables, saying: "The kingdom of heaven is like a king who prepared a wedding banquet for his son. He sent his servants to those who had been invited to the banquet to tell them to come, but they refused to come.

" ' "Then he sent some more servants and said, 'Tell those who have been invited that I have prepared my dinner: My oxen and fattened cattle have been butchered, and everything is ready. Come to the wedding banquet.'

" ' "But they paid no attention and went off—one to his field, another to his business. The rest seized his servants, mistreated them and killed them. The king was enraged. He sent his army and destroyed those murderers and burned their city.

" ' "Then he said to his servants, 'The wedding banquet is ready, but those I invited did not deserve to come. Go to the street corners and invite to the banquet anyone you find.' So the servants went out into the streets and gathered all the people they could find, both good and bad, and the wedding hall was filled with guests.

" ' "But when the king came in to see the guests, he noticed a man there who was not wearing wedding clothes. 'Friend,' he asked, 'how did you get in here without wedding clothes?' The man was speechless.

" ' "Then the king told the attendants, 'Tie him hand and foot, and throw him outside, into the darkness, where there will be weeping and gnashing of teeth' " ' " (Matthew 22:1–13, NIV).

Thomas stopped reading and looked up. "Why was the guest thrown out?" he asked. "What made the difference?"

"He didn't have wedding clothes," Lyn replied quickly.

"That's right. And who gave the guests their wedding clothes?"

"The king," Tildy said. "It was the custom in those days for the hosts to provide the wedding clothes."

Thomas nodded eagerly, as though his listeners were a classroom of especially bright pupils. "Yes, yes. And what are the wedding clothes if not the righteousness of Christ? Do you see? The difference was not in who the guest was. He wasn't smarter or gentler or more generous than the others. It doesn't even say whether he was good—both the good and the bad were invited. The difference was in what he didn't have. He hadn't accepted the righteousness of Christ. He expected to attend the wedding feast entirely on his own merit, but that was impossible. At the wedding he needed what we need in the judgment—something to cover him."

"So, what you're saying is that we're not on trial at the judgment," Lyn said slowly, as though testing an idea that was just occurring to her. "If we have accepted Christ, then He is on trial, because it's His character covering us, not our own. If He had any fault, then we wouldn't be saved. But because He's perfect, we can stand through the judgment."

"That's right. During the judgment, God puts a seal on our choice—whether we have accepted or rejected Him."

"I realize He's God, so I suppose He can just know that, but *how* does He know?" Lyn asked.

" 'By their fruits ye shall know them,' " Thomas quoted off the cuff (Matthew 7:20, KJV). "It's our works that tell whether or not we have accepted Christ."

"Our works can't save us," Tildy retorted, her lower lip quivering defiantly.

"You're right. I never said they could save us." Thomas thumped the Bible with his index finger. "If works were what we needed for salvation, Jesus wouldn't have had to die for us. But in the judgment, our works will show who has accepted Christ's righteousness and who hasn't.

"Jesus said that what we do for the least of our brothers, we do for Him. We can never do enough—feed enough people, clothe enough people, visit enough people, help enough people—to save ourselves. Instead, we do these things out of gratitude to Christ for saving us."

Maddie glanced up at Lyn and found that her daughter was sobbing silently into her hands. "I feel so dirty," she wept. "I've been so selfish, so self-centered. Will you pray for me?"

"Of course we will," Thomas exclaimed. He dropped onto his knees, and Tildy followed rather shakily. Maddie also slipped from her chair onto her knees beside her daughter, and she held Lyn as Thomas prayed.

"Lord, we come to You today with grateful hearts. We thank You for each person gathered here. We thank You for saving us. We thank You for Your infinite mercy. We ask You to be with each person here. Draw us closer to You. We want to know You better so we can love You better."

"And God," Lyn broke in with a sob, "please forgive me. I've led a terrible life. I've done so many things against You. I'm so very sorry. Thank You for saving me and for accepting me even though I'm sinful. Show me how to be a better person."

THE THIRD COMING

"Help me to rely on You," Tildy prayed when Lyn finished. "Help me to trust You. Help me to believe that You're in control so I can have peace. And be with my cat. Please help her paw to heal."

An occasional "Thank You, Lord" and "Praise You, Lord" broke the quiet. Then Maddie said, "Lord, I thank You for my daughter, Lyn. I thank You for giving her a tender heart. And despite the circumstances, I thank You for the child she carries. I hope that we'll have the opportunity to raise him or her in heaven, far from this wicked world. I thank You for the wonderful husband You gave me, and for my son. I know he had his problems, but I'm still asking You for a miracle, hoping that he made his peace with You before he died. Thank You for bringing us to this place to wait out this time of trouble with Your people and for watching over us all here. Amen."

A chorus of "Amens" followed, and the group all rose slowly to their feet. Thomas put his arm around Lyn's shoulders and offered her a handkerchief. "God loves you, Lyn," he said softly. "God loves you more than you could ever know."

Lyn blew her nose loudly and nodded, but she didn't say anything.

"I think you should go lie down for a bit, honey," Maddie said. There were great black half circles beneath Lyn's eyes, and her face was pale. But there was a new light in her eyes. It was, Maddie realized suddenly, relief.

"I think I will. Thanks, Mom." Lyn hugged her fiercely. "I love you, Mom," she whispered. "Thank you for always believing in me."

"I love you too, honey." Maddie forced the words past the lump in her throat. "Nothing will ever change that. Now, go and get some rest. You look tired."

Maddie watched Lyn cross the room to go to the cabin they shared with two other families. She felt such love and gratitude well up inside her that she could hardly breathe. "Thank You, God, for my girl. Please, please save my son," she whispered.

As happy as she was knowing that she would soon see Daniel again and that Lyn's heart was now right with God, a deep sadness skirted the edge of her happiness, clouding it. Her joy would be complete if Brian would join them at the Second Coming. If only. Maddie heaved a tired sigh and picked up the sewing, her fingers working while she prayed.

BOOK ONE:
THE BEGINNING OF THE END

CHAPTER THIRTEEN

It was difficult to tell which season it was by the weather. Hot and cold, rainy and snowy, it all came together. Sometimes a brief cold spell would decimate all the vegetation and then a quick hot spell would partially revive it. Maddie figured it must be getting close to fall, but the leaves didn't change color as they normally did. Instead, they turned brown, shriveled up, and fell off the trees, forming a crunchy carpet through which people trudged between the cabins.

One morning, Maddie and Lyn entered the common room to find a large group gathered around Pastor Mitchell, who was motioning for quiet. Thomas was standing by the door, and he helped make room for them. "Good, you're here," he said. "We're trying to get everyone in to hear this. There's news."

Maddie felt a flutter of excitement in the pit of her stomach. Although there were generally several newsworthy items each week, they were becoming standard fare: more wars breaking out, odd weather patterns, viruses mutating from known varieties and becoming so "hot" that they killed entire cities before disappearing as quickly as they arrived. But she knew that the calling of a special meeting meant something extraordinary had occurred.

"Brothers and sisters, can I have your attention please?" Pastor Mitchell held up his hands for silence, and the low hum flowing through the room stuttered and died. "We have just heard over the radio that peace has been declared in the Middle East." A murmur of astonishment rippled across the room. "Terms are being negotiated, but all parties are willing. One item of supreme interest to us is that the temple, which was formerly held by the Ibhar Militia group, has been returned to the Israeli government. Israel announced today that they intend to dedicate the temple in celebration of the peace treaty."

"What does that mean?" Maddie asked Thomas in a whisper. "Why is it important?"

Thomas explained, "The special red cow always used for the temple sacrifices became extinct long ago. The Israelis couldn't dedicate the temple without it. Through modern technology, they were able to use some DNA to re-create the breed. But immediately after they did so, extremists seized the temple and the area surrounding it. The extremists have held that area ever since, so the Israelis have never been able to dedicate the temple."

"Why is that important?"

"One theory is that Satan will use the dedication of the temple to deceive people. Whenever a temple was dedicated in Old Testament times, God's glory descended and He 'lived' in the temple. Satan could easily masquerade as the glory of God. We'll know soon enough, because when they dedicate the temple, it won't be God who inhabits it. If something or someone does, we'll know who it is."

Maddie nodded thoughtfully. Thomas's explanation put a whole new light on things.

"Pope Paul Sanctus is flying out today and will be giving the dedication speech," Pastor Mitchell was saying. "They hope to have everything ready by the end of the week."

"A week to negotiate a peace it's taken decades to secure?" Maddie gasped in astonishment.

Thomas nodded gravely. "Haven't we been told that in the end, things will happen swiftly?"

"I can't wait," Lyn said, a half-smile on her lips as she caressed her growing abdomen. "I want to see Jesus." Her whole face glowed with the thought. "It will take me years to thank Him enough for forgiving me."

For the rest of that week, the common room was fuller than usual. All those who had a few minutes to spare gathered around the radio as they waited for news about the temple dedication. The event was being hashed and rehashed by commentators, political and religious leaders, presidents, and even interested celebrities—particularly the ones starring in religious programs and movies. It seemed as though everyone had something to say about it, and nearly everything people said was positive.

By coincidence—or providence, the world collectively believed—one of the red cows in the special breeding program in Israel was perfectly spotless and precisely the correct age. The authorities had identified it and were feeding it a special diet. More than one person speculated that this dedication of the temple—and with it, a rededication of the world to the commands of God—would end the bad weather, plagues, and rogue viruses. The consensus was that God had been trying to get the world's attention, and now He finally had it. Everyone wanted to know what He had to say. More importantly, they wanted Him to know that they were listening.

As the week of preparation began, something else unexpected happened. People decided that if they were present when God's glory filled the temple in Israel, should that really take place, it was possible, even probable, that they would be healed. So, sick and injured people determined to reach Israel in time for the dedication of the temple were clogging airports around the world. By midweek, they had filled to capacity all the hotels and other accommodations in and around Jerusalem. And by the day before the anticipated event, people were camping out in sleeping bags as close to the temple as they could get.

On the day of the dedication, everyone at the little community in the woods gathered in the common room to listen to the radio. The air quickly grew stale, and Maddie found herself squeezed into one corner, pinned to the wall by the people pressing close. She breathed slowly and called for someone to open a window. Then the radio crackled to life, and the room became so silent that she could hear Pastor Mitchell's asthmatic wheezes from across the room.

"This is John Smart beginning live coverage of the temple dedication service in Jerusalem for World Public Radio," a tinny voice said as a satellite conveyed the reporter's words around the world. "Over a billion people have converged on this small corner of the earth. Bank upon bank of people surround the temple, making it impossible for anyone inside to leave.

"Officials have placed the most infirm spectators in the courtyard of the temple, closest to where the ceremony will take place. Pope Paul Sanctus and other world leaders, along with Rabbi Solomon Shalom, who represents the sovereign state of Israel, have gathered inside the temple for the service that begins at any moment. Rabbi Shalom is addressing the crowd now."

A voice-over brought a stream of measured Hebrew nearly drowned out by a translator with a badly affected Hebrew accent giving the English version of the rabbi's words. "I greet you in the name of Yahweh, the Creator who made all things and will make all things new again," the translator said. "We gather here today to witness a great act, a holy act, which has not been performed in Israel since ancient times. I am honored to have such distinguished guests with us, and I ask them to speak a few words on this very special occasion."

One by one, the leaders conveyed their hopes that this dedication service would demonstrate to God that they but waited to do His bidding. They expressed sorrow for their conduct, and they promised a worldwide repentance and turning from their wickedness if God would only draw back His hand of punishment from them. The pope spoke last, in his native Italian, with his own translator. Though he was an old man and had to be supported on both sides in order to stand to give his address, he spoke the longest and the most passionately, begging Mary to have mercy on the world and appease the wrath of her dear Son and His Father.

After a brief silence during which the radio's static crackled with intensity throughout the room, John Smart said, "Now they are preparing to slaughter the bull. Interestingly enough, media sources have nicknamed the bull Penny—in part, for its copper color, but primarily as a shortened form of Repentance. Animal rights activists have staged protests across the globe in a bid to save Penny's life. And now, yes, it's confirmed, Penny has been sacrificed according to Jewish tradition. In only a few moments we should know whether God, or whoever is in charge of the universe, accepts the sacrifice."

A tense silence seemed to stretch forever. Then Smart's excited voice boomed more loudly than before from the speakers. He was speaking so fast that Maddie had trouble understanding him. "Fire has come down from the sky," he was saying, stumbling over his words—his professionalism abandoned in the excitement. "A great ball of fire entered the temple and consumed the bull as it lay on the altar. There's absolutely nothing left but a little pile of smoldering ashes. And now, wait, there's a man—a man shining as though he were on fire himself—coming through the curtain before the Most Holy Place. He's holding up his hands, and all the leaders are bowing down before him. I'm not a Christian myself, folks, but I think—I think it must be Jesus Christ!"

74

A mélange of confusion permeated the airwaves for a few minutes. People were shouting—a great roar that temporarily drowned out any chance for intelligent commentary. As suddenly as the noise had begun, it stopped, and a perfect silence followed. And then a beautiful, melodious, deep, comforting voice full of peace and reassurance flooded through the small room. Maddie felt herself shake as if she were suddenly cold. She knew exactly who was speaking.

"Peace, brothers and sisters. I bring you peace. I have traveled from the courts of my heavenly father to give you this message: I will forgive you, but you must demonstrate your repentance by putting away that which is abhorrent to me. I am angry with the people who claim to be my followers yet who do not obey my commands. These people profane Sunday, my holy day, and cause my true children to question me. I will not tolerate this behavior any longer. They must be purged from among you as vermin."

The voice had grown thunderous with anger, but then it stopped. When it began again, it was soft and full of sunshine. "I want my children, my true children, to have peace. That is why I have come. Come to me, you who have carried heavy burdens, and I will give you my peace. Now is the time for everyone to have peace if they will but follow me."

Smart's voice broke in as cheering erupted in the background. "I have received the incredible report from our sister stations worldwide that the preceding message, given by Jesus, the son of God, was received in the language of every country we reach without the need for translation. Folks, this is staggering. But wait! A woman has just appeared by Jesus' side! She is shining like he is—as though they are both on fire!"

"My beloved people," a woman's voice said, so beautiful and comforting that Maddie felt herself relax her guard for a moment. "Listen to my son, for great is the wrath of his father. We are trying to save you from the terrible punishment he will visit upon you if you do not heed our words. Listen, my people, and obey."

John Smart broke in again. "Pope Paul Sanctus has informed us that this woman is Mary, the mother of Jesus, and a holy person if there ever was one. She and Jesus are now moving into the crowd. Somehow, they can move freely through the mass of people. And everyone they touch is healed! It's incredible! The blind can see, the paralyzed can walk, people are leaping out of their wheelchairs—it's the most fantastic sight I've ever witnessed!"

Smart's voice broke with emotion. "This has been a great day, a very great day. It will go down in the history of the world, and I am honored that I was allowed to witness it firsthand." He tried to go on, but only his quiet sobs echoed through the still room. "I believe, I believe . . ." he was sobbing as the transmission was suddenly cut off and classical music began.

Pastor Mitchell switched off the radio. "I think everyone in this room has a clear grasp of what just happened," he said soberly.

"But what if he's right? What if it really is Jesus?" Maddie craned her neck and could see that it was Tildy who was speaking, her cat hugged tight to her chest, her face anxious.

"If Jesus were in Jerusalem," Pastor Mitchell said gently, "we would all know because the Bible says, 'Behold, He is coming with clouds, and every eye will see Him.' [Revelation 1:7, NKJV.] We didn't see Him, so He isn't here yet."

Tildy nodded but was still clearly worried. Maddie wished she could reach the older woman to put her arms around her. The tension of waiting for something to happen was wearing on all of them. She wanted to believe that Jesus was there in Jerusalem and that all earth's trouble would soon cease and there would be peace. But she knew it wasn't true. Peace would come only in heaven. And when Jesus did return to earth, no one would wonder if it really was Him.

BOOK ONE:
THE BEGINNING OF THE END

CHAPTER FOURTEEN

There was no real winter that year. December arrived with a blast of warm air and a continuous light mist that kept everything soaked most of the time. A dense fog had settled over the countryside, though how far it extended in any direction they could only guess. While the temperature outside was relatively warm, everything indoors was chilly with dampness. Nothing ever really dried out. Thomas pointed out that they would soon have a mold problem on their hands if nothing changed.

Maddie spent most of her free time trying to keep some of the baby clothes dry because Lyn's baby was due any day. Lyn was extremely uncomfortable, her hands and feet swollen and painful. There was no doctor among the community residents, but the nurse who looked after their medical complaints as best she could confided in Maddie that she was worried about Lyn's blood pressure and ordered her on strict bed rest.

Lyn complied because she was concerned about the baby. But she chafed at the inactivity, and even the steady stream of visitors who read to her and played games with her didn't alleviate the boredom of staying in a damp, chilly bed twenty-four hours a day.

Thomas was a regular visitor, and Maddie began to question the reason for his kindness. "Where's your family?" she asked him one day when Lyn had dozed off and they were otherwise alone in the room.

"Most of them are in Illinois," he said, a faraway look in his eyes. "I came here to go to school."

"Are they believers?"

He shook his head sadly. "I don't know. I don't think so. I certainly wasn't raised with any deep convictions of faith. I had a friend in college who was on fire for the Lord. It was through him that I came to know Jesus."

"Where is he now?" Maddie asked. She wondered if Thomas knew where her questions were headed.

"I don't know. He decided to become a missionary. I haven't heard from him in years."

"And you have no one else?"

Thomas hesitated before answering. "I did have. I had a girlfriend. She was such a wonderful, caring, sweet person that I thought it was only a matter of time before she became a Christian. But she couldn't see the need for it. She was the kind of person who was always doing something thoughtful for someone else. She visited people in nursing homes and prisons. She was in a singing program for patients at the local hospital. She was always doing something." He laughed ruefully. "At the time, I accused her of liking to help other people more than she liked spending time with me."

"Maybe she already was a Christian," Maddie suggested.

Thomas shrugged. "I'm not going to judge her. The true condition of her heart is between her and God."

" 'By their fruits ye shall know them,' " quoted Maddie (Matthew 7:20).

"That's true," Thomas agreed. "I've thought about that a lot—you know, the relation between works and faith. And I think that was the missing link for her. She had works. She was a decent person. But she didn't have faith. Works can't save you. Only faith can save you.

"Ellie was very independent. She didn't like to rely on anyone. She wanted to do it all herself. But you can't save yourself. Only Jesus can save you."

Maddie waited, and Thomas continued hesitantly. "I'm very fond of your daughter."

"I guessed as much. What happened to Ellie?"

"She left because she wasn't comfortable with church. She didn't mind that I 'had religion,' as she called it. But the whole business of organized religion turned her off. She wanted to be a free spirit and worship her higher power in her own way. I haven't seen her in years."

Thomas looked up, a slight smile on his lips. "I'm not trying to kid you or myself. I know we're living in the last days and that Lyn is pregnant with another man's child. I'm not going to ask her out on a date or suggest we get married quickly in case we all die tomorrow. I just . . . I like her. I like her a lot. She has a childlike innocence about her relationship with God that I find very refreshing. The Bible says there won't be any marriage in heaven, but I guess I just want to say that I'll be proud to have you both as my friends."

"Thomas!" Michael called, interrupting them. He had pushed the door of the hut open and poked his face inside. "Pastor Mitchell is calling an emergency meeting. They've found us, and we think they'll be moving in soon."

Thomas followed Michael wordlessly, leaving Maddie to gape after them in shock. They'd been found! It was only a matter of time now. For months, they'd been hearing about the rounding up of the "insubordinates," who were "displeasing God" and "jeopardizing peace on earth." Not only were these people taken—thousands of them hounded out of caves and from hiding places—but they were also executed immediately as the authorities sought to appease God and avert more catastrophes.

Maddie turned to Lyn, a stricken look on her face, and found Lyn's dark eyes on her. Then Lyn said, "Mom, I'm having contractions."

"What?"

Maddie struggled to get her mind around the fact that not only were they about to be taken and executed, but now Lyn was in labor. "Dear God, please have mercy on us!" she begged.

"Mom, it's OK. It's natural, remember?"

Maddie fought to pull her lips into a smile. "You're right, honey. It's just a case of pre-grandma jitters. You're perfectly right. Everything will be fine. I'm going to get Hannah to help. I'll be right back."

Hannah examined Lyn, her lips tight and her jaw clenched. The nurse knew the implications of what was happening too, but Maddie had cautioned her against telling Lyn. It made no sense to terrify a teenage girl who was in labor. Nothing they could do would change a thing. They must do their best and rely on God to get them through it.

"You're doing well, Lyn," Hannah said. "But you'll need to fortify yourself. It could be a long wait. First babies like to take their time."

Lyn's red, sweaty face beamed at her as she struggled through another long, hard contraction. "I—can't—wait—to—see—my—baby," she said between pants.

Hannah gave Lyn's hand a squeeze and exchanged knowing looks with Maddie. "That's what every mother says."

"That's right," Maddie chipped in with forced cheerfulness. "I said the same thing when I was in labor with you and with Brian."

Every time a contraction gripped Lyn, Maddie felt as though her own insides were being painfully compressed. She would rather have gone through the labor herself if doing so could have spared Lyn the agony she was enduring.

Near midnight, a knock on the door called Maddie away from Lyn's side for a moment. She straightened up and pushed the door open a crack.

"How is she?" Thomas's face was white in the darkness.

"It's almost over."

"So is our freedom," Thomas said. "They're beginning to move in. There's really nothing we can do. There's nowhere to go. They have us surrounded."

Even as he spoke, they heard the popcornlike sound of distant machine-gun fire and muffled screams that followed. Thomas grabbed Maddie's shoulders, pushed her back into the little cabin, and followed her in. Then, closing the door, he threw his back against it and braced himself.

Lyn barely noticed that he was there, and Hannah didn't bother to protest. She knew as well as they did what was happening outside. "Push," she instructed Lyn. "I'll have the head out in a moment. Wait now . . . wait . . . Let me ease the shoulders out. Good girl! Push again."

Thomas looked away respectfully, but Maddie watched in wonder as a small, slippery baby emerged from her daughter's body. "It's a boy," Hannah announced. She laid the squirming, bawling baby in Lyn's arms just as something crashed against the door with a great, thundering noise.

Thomas threw himself backwards to prevent whoever was outside from entering, but the next moment a blast of machine gun fire from outside punched through the door and found its mark. Thomas slumped to the ground without a sound. He cradled his abdomen in his arms while his life's blood flowed out and made a dark puddle on the floor.

Maddie screamed and threw herself across Lyn and the baby. Then the floor began to rock violently, and the roof of the cabin, though solidly constructed, slid sideways as the walls leaned drunkenly. The great gaping hole above them revealed a rainbow of color in the sky. It had become as bright as noon on a sunny day in the winter, and great flashes of lightning seared their eyes. Maddie's gaze was riveted to the sight unfolding above her.

A great voice, like the sound of waves crashing on a rocky shore, said, "It is done." The very heavens shook, and the earth with them. The shaking grew so intense that Maddie feared for Lyn. She gripped her tightly, and the baby bawled between them. Outside the cabin, the wind shrieked with such fury that it sounded like the voices of a multitude of demons unleashed upon the earth.

Clouds raced across the sky, and as Maddie watched, a rip appeared, revealing a bright and shining star, the brilliance of which competed with the sun. The sight of the star filled Maddie with hope and joy, though she couldn't say why. Then she noticed in the east a small black cloud the size of a man's fist hurling toward the earth. As it grew in size, its darkness became light, and the details became increasingly clear—until Maddie could see that it really was a great white cloud that enveloped Jesus in glory and majesty. A rainbow arced above Him, He was treading on a mass of fire, and millions of angels surrounded Him—all of whom were singing and praising God.

"Lyn, look, look!" Maddie exclaimed as she helped Lyn to sit up so she could see the awesome sight.

"Who will be able to stand?" Hannah cried, voicing the question that Maddie herself felt as she looked up at Jesus in His perfection and glory. For a moment, the angels stopped singing, and a great and terrible silence fell over the entire earth. Maddie thought her heart would stop beating while she waited to hear the words for which she prayed.

"My grace is sufficient for you," Jesus said, and He seemed to be looking directly at Maddie—though later, all those Maddie spoke to said He seemed to be looking directly at them too. Maddie hugged Lyn, overcome with joy. The angels began to sing again, and the cloud drew closer to the earth.

The earth began rolling once more. The booming thunder and the sound of mountains crumbling were deafening. And Maddie could hear the screams of people begging the rocks to fall on them. But inside the cabin there was peace.

"Awake, awake, awake, ye that sleep in the dust, and arise!" Jesus shouted. Beside them, Thomas stirred and sat up slowly, trying to take in everything at once.

"Thomas!" Maddie sobbed joyfully. "Oh, Thomas! Look! Jesus has come for us. We are saved!"

He stood and with cautious fingers probed the bullet holes riddling his body. Then he gazed with adoration at Jesus, who looked straight at him and said, "Greater love hath no man than this, that a man lay down his life for his friends."

Instantly, Maddie, Lyn, Thomas, Hannah, and Lyn's baby were transformed, their earthly bodies gone. Now they were glorified, shining, and perfect. Maddie was amazed. She glowed as though she were burning in a white-hot fire, yet she felt perfectly cool. A shimmering robe that seemed to be made of liquid fire draped around her, and she saw that others were wearing a similar garment. The surroundings seemed incredibly clear to her, as though before she'd looked at them through smoke. She noticed details she hadn't seen before. Colors were all more intense, scents more pungent. All her senses were heightened.

And she was shocked at how clear her mind was. She felt as though a heavy blanket had been lifted off her brain. Before, she had always been preoccupied, taking in only a tiny portion of life. Now she was keenly aware of everything. Every sensation, every nuance, every action had greater meaning. The transformation was of such a magnitude that she could never have explained it to anyone who hadn't experienced it.

Suddenly, Maddie felt a sense of lightness, and she realized that they were all rising through the air. She didn't feel insecure, as though she were flying. Instead, she felt confident, as though she had simply learned a new way of navigating through space. When she looked back and saw the earth shrinking beneath her, twisting and writhing as if it were in agony, she didn't feel fearful of the height but exhilarated by it.

"Maddie!" She recognized Daniel's voice before she saw him. An angel was leading him to where she stood with Lyn and the others. No longer was he gaunt and hollow. He glowed as she did, his form perfect as it was always meant to be.

"Daniel!" she exclaimed, and she threw her arms around his neck and clung to him fiercely. "Daniel, I'm so happy to see you! I tried to visit you in the prison, but they said . . . they said—"

"Daddy!" Lyn burrowed into their embrace. "Daddy, you're here! Look, you have a grandson."

Daniel clutched them both and drank in the sight of his first grandchild with tears of happiness in his eyes. "My family! I thank my wonderful Savior you are all here. If only my son were here, my joy would be complete." In vain, they turned to see if some angel might be leading Brian to them, but none came.

"Who is this?" Daniel asked, wiping his eyes and smiling at Thomas.

"A friend," Maddie said. "A very good friend indeed. Someone who gave his life trying to save us."

"I'm pleased to meet you, sir," Thomas said as he took Daniel's hand and shook it warmly. "You have a wonderful family."

"I am a fortunate man indeed," Daniel agreed. "And now you shall join my family."

"I'd be honored. I have no family of my own."

Around them, the throng of righteous began to make their way toward the glorious chariot of Jesus as it ascended toward the New Jerusalem. The wheels and the wings of the chariot cried, "Holy!" and the angels returned their shout. "Holy, holy, holy, Lord God almighty!"

And the redeemed answered, "Alleluia!"

Maddie thought that all the happiness possible was contained in that one word. The pain and fear and awfulness of earth had passed away. They were on their way to heaven, where they would live for a thousand years.

As they stood among the throng, an angel descended toward earth with a great key in one hand and a heavy chain and lock in another. There he laid his hands on the most hideous creature Maddie had ever seen. A great hulking demon he was, stoop-shouldered though he had been tall, with a leering countenance and defiant attitude. Great wings drooped behind him, and Maddie realized that this was Satan.

The two grappled for a moment, but the angel easily overpowered Satan. Then he bound him with the chain, marked his forehead, and cast him down to the earth. And the angel proclaimed, "You shall deceive no one till the thousand years are fulfilled."

At those words, a long, anguished, angry howl arose from the earth. Glancing down, Maddie could see Satan crawling amidst the desolation and ruins of earth, consumed with rage and despair. He was doomed to walk the earth until the New Jerusalem returned and sin had its final and absolute end.

Maddie turned resolutely away from the scene below and looked up, over the throngs of the redeemed, toward Jesus. She slipped beneath Daniel's arm and walked close to him. Those redeemed from earth raised their voices in songs of praise, and she joined them, singing with all the power of her new lungs. The sound all of them produced was magnificent. It swelled and accompanied them as they moved upward. Lyn and Thomas followed with the baby, and around them rose layers upon layers of sound—all praise, giving glory to Jesus, who had saved them!

BOOK TWO:

THE JUDGMENT

BOOK TWO:
THE JUDGMENT

CHAPTER FIFTEEN

With the glow of the earth beneath them and the brightness of Jesus ahead, the gathered multitude began to journey toward heaven. It was a journey unlike any Maddie had ever taken or even conceived of. They traveled on the very air around them. They walked, yet it wasn't really walking. They didn't get tired, so they never needed to stop for rest breaks. They did, however, pause to admire extraordinary celestial sights and meet the glorious beings who inhabited other planets along the way.

Jesus said they could come back later and visit as long as they liked, but He was eager to reach home. His excitement was so obvious that Maddie felt herself caught up in it. In a small way, it reminded her of times when one of her children had made something special for her at school and couldn't wait to show her.

Thinking of those times brought Brian to her mind. "When we reach heaven, we'll ask Jesus," Daniel said, as though reading her thoughts.

"How did you know what I was thinking?" Maddie asked in wonder.

Daniel reflected before replying. "I just knew. It came to me. Just like I know what you're thinking right now."

"What?"

"You're thinking how glad you are that I'm here and how very handsome I look—not at all like the ragbag you visited so often in prison." His face was serious but there was laughter in his eyes, and since Maddie had purposely filled her mind with Lyn's child to test him, she knew he was teasing.

"I wasn't," she said, and laughed. "I was thinking of Redeemed. But you're right. I couldn't be happier that you're here."

It was Thomas who had suggested to Lyn that she name her baby Redeemed. They all agreed that the name was perfect. The child was a marvel to them all. He was so strong and so healthy, so bright and alert, that he seemed months older than he was. Already, he appeared to recognize the ones closest to him. He didn't nurse at his mother's breast but ate the food they all received, a thin wafer of honey sweetness, accompanied by clear, sweet water. "Manna," the angel had explained, smiling, when he brought the food to them the first time.

"I am so happy and full of energy that I could run all the way to heaven and not get tired!" Thomas exclaimed. Gladness filled his voice and suffused his face, and Maddie felt her own joy increase to see his.

The trip to heaven took seven days, but the time passed so swiftly that to Maddie it seemed like only a few hours. Songs were raised continually, and taken up and carried the length of the procession. Now and then, an angel would bring to Maddie or the others someone they knew, and there would be a joyful reunion. Debbie was the first.

"Debbie! I'm so happy to see you! I've prayed for you constantly since I saw you last. What happened to you?" Maddie hugged her friend with enthusiasm when an angel reunited them.

"Maddie! How I longed to see you! I asked Jewel if he knew where you were, and he did!" Debbie nodded to indicate the angel, who had stepped aside while they spoke.

To Maddie, her friend looked the same, yet different. Debbie was glorified, like Maddie, but she had changed in some other way too. Perhaps it was that she was also more refined. Her speech was certainly not coarse, as it had been on earth.

In answer to Maddie's question, Debbie said, "You know, somehow what happened on earth doesn't seem terribly important now. I was taken just a few days after I saw you last. But I wasn't killed. They brought me to the prison—you know, the one where Daniel was. It was extremely overcrowded, and we suffered unbearably. However," Debbie was quick to add, "I am so happy now that it seems such a small thing.

"I met up with my friends in the prison—the ones I told you about, the Raynards. They'd been my neighbors on earth. In fact, it was through their influence that I became a Christian in the first place. We stuck together. Without them, I would have been very lonely. I didn't know another soul, though people were very kind to each other. Well, the Christians were kind. The others made life very hard for all of us.

"Anyway, at the end, the guards were ordered to kill us all, but when they raised their guns to shoot us, the guns broke in half. Then Jesus came, and they begged us to save them, but of course we couldn't."

After a pause, Debbie said, her eyes shining, "I want to thank you,

Maddie, for helping me so much on earth. I would have given up a thousand times if it hadn't been for you and my other Christian friends. I felt so worthless and so guilty about my life before I became a Christian. It was hard to understand how much Jesus really loves me. Even now, I'm not sure I understand completely." She laughed. "But I guess that's what eternity's for, right?"

After Debbie had gone, Maddie contemplated what she'd said. While she remembered occasions when she'd encouraged Debbie, at the time she hadn't understood the influence of her actions and words. It was sobering to think what might have happened to Debbie if Maddie hadn't taken the time—and she rarely had any to spare—to help her friend get back on the right path.

Maddie's thoughts turned to Jean, and she wondered where she was. Jewel, the angel who had brought Debbie to see her, was still nearby. He strode purposefully, his golden face shining and his majestic wings folded behind him. He was tall, incredibly tall, and Maddie felt like a child standing next to him.

"Excuse me." She tugged on the sleeve of Jewel's robe, and slowly Jewel's beautiful face turned toward her. He smiled and said, "You'll 'grow up' too when you've eaten of the tree of life. The final lingering traces of sin will be wiped away, and you will all appear in the beauty and splendor of the Master Himself. In your minds, souls, and bodies, you will reflect His perfect image."

"How did you know what I was wondering?" Maddie asked. "Can you read my mind?"

Jewel laughed with rich, ringing tones that sounded like the deep-throated peals of bells in a steeple tower. "No, my little one. I can't read your thoughts. But I've had centuries of studying the ways of humankind. So, when people stand close to me and stare up at me as you did, I know what question is in their minds, whether or not they ask. It's only natural for you to wonder."

"You're right, I did wonder," Maddie admitted. "But I was going to ask a different question."

Jewel's chiseled eyebrows, which framed eyes of sapphire, arched. "Oh? What is that? You see, I can't read your mind now, or I would answer before you could ask."

"I haven't seen my good friend Jean King. Would you point her out to me so that I can visit with her for a few minutes? Or would you take me to her?"

Maddie felt, as much as saw, the angel's sadness. "I'm sorry," he said, "but that is not possible. There are questions that have no answers here. When we reach the holy city, you'll be able to speak with Jesus and to look through the books yourself so that you may be satisfied regarding the cases of people who aren't here."

"She's . . . not here?" Maddie faltered, unbelieving. "Are you sure? There must be hundreds of Jean Kings in the world, after all. Surely more than one was saved—maybe the one I'm asking about?"

"I am so very sorry for your loss," the angel murmured gravely. "I know precisely the person you speak of. She is not here. When you have looked over the books, you will understand why she couldn't be among the redeemed. In heaven, the judgment of the wicked will take place, and you will not only understand but you will help decide her punishment."

Maddie considered this. If Jean and Brian weren't among those ascending to heaven, then they were among the wicked who had died and remained on earth. The redeemed would spend the next thousand years participating in their judgment. That meant that she and Daniel, Lyn, Thomas, and all the others would determine, with Jesus, what punishment should be meted out against them according to their deeds.

"You won't understand this matter before you've looked at the books," the angel said gently. "You know so little of the experiences, motives, and minds of others. But God, the Master, knows all. You must trust the Master to reveal everything in its proper time and place. Use the time you have until then to reunite with those who are here and to give glory and thanks to King Jesus for saving you."

Maddie nodded and said, "Thank you for telling me."

Jewel placed a massive hand on her shoulder, engulfing it. "The Master wanted to save you all. There is room and to spare in heaven, and there will be on the new earth too. He did all in His power to bid His children to come. And He gave them every tool they needed to remain faithful followers until He could bring them safely to heaven.

"But the one thing the Master respects above all is a free will. He will never, never force His will upon those who don't want to receive it. The path that leads to Jesus the Master is love and obedience. These, plus trust and faith, bind the heart of the believer to Him in love without coercion. Those who don't follow the true path can't reach the same destination as those who do."

"I understand," Maddie whispered. "I know Jesus won't force anyone to follow Him, and I know that even if He did, they wouldn't be happy here. I just can't help but wish some of the people I know—Jean, my son, and others—I can't help wishing they had listened to His voice and followed Him. I want them to be here."

"So does the Master, little sister," Jewel said sorrowfully. "He loves them more than any of us can comprehend. You've seen the scars on His hands and feet. You know what He gave for them so they could be here. But He won't force them to accept salvation."

"How long will we travel to reach heaven?" Maddie asked after they had walked in silence for a while.

"It takes seven days to reach the Sea of Glass," Jewel replied. Then he waved a hand toward the road ahead and said, "But you can see that we're nearly there."

"Nearly there?" Maddie cried. "But we couldn't have been traveling seven days already. Why, we never even slept!"

"And you won't sleep," the angel replied, "for there is no night in heaven. Look! The Sea of Glass stretches before us. We have arrived. I must go now; I have duties to perform. Blessings on you, little sister. I am very glad you chose to be here."

Jewel was gone in an instant, and Maddie turned to Daniel, who had been walking quietly by her side during their conversation. "Did you hear what Jewel said?" she asked.

"Yes." Daniel's voice was sore with the ache of sadness. "Yes, I heard. We'll speak with Jesus. There may yet be hope."

Maddie slipped her hand into Daniel's as they approached the Sea of Glass, and for the moment, they forgot everything else but the glorious sight in front of them. Then God the Father spoke, saying words Maddie remembered reading in Isaiah, "The sun shall no longer be your light by day, nor for brightness shall the moon give light to you; but the Lord will be to you an everlasting light, and your God your glory. Your sun shall no longer go down, nor shall your moon withdraw itself; for the Lord will be your everlasting light, and the days of your mourning shall be ended. Also, your people shall all be righteous; they shall inherit the land forever. The branch of My planting, the work of My hands, that I may be glorified. A little one shall become a thousand and a small one a strong nation." (See Isaiah 60:19–22.)

Jesus turned to them as they formed a giant square on the Sea. Angels beside Him held crowns that He began to place on their heads, speaking to each one as He did so. When He extended Maddie's crown, she saw that it was a golden circle studded with stars. The stars shone with fire—not like diamonds, but even brighter, as though fire leaping within them lit them from the inside. And each star bore a name. Maddie could see *Debbie, Lyn, Daniel,* and many others written on the stars on her crown. They were the names of all the people to whom she had presented the truth and who had been saved.

Maddie noticed all these things in an instant, and then she looked at the face of Jesus with gratitude and love. A tender smile crinkled the corners of His mouth, and He embraced her after He laid the crown on her head. "My daughter, welcome to the home I have prepared for you," He said.

"Thank You, Jesus. Thank You so much. Thank You for everything," Maddie said, and she felt tears shining in her eyes.

Jesus reached out to wipe the tears away. "It was for *you* that I sacrificed My life, for the atonement of *your* sins," He said, His eyes intent on hers, while Maddie looked at Him enraptured. "You are worth every drop of blood and every moment of the agonizing time I spent separated from My Father. For you alone I would have given My life."

When all the redeemed had received a crown, a harp, and a palm branch that signified victory, they looked to Jesus. He raised His arm and grabbed hold of one of the pearl gates. "You who have washed your robes in My blood and stood stiffly for My truth, enter in," He said.

As one, the mighty gathering marched across the Sea of Glass to the city. Maddie waved her palm branch and sang with the others as they were swept along through the gates. The loud cry was taken up and carried like a wave. It sounded and resounded until it seemed like thousands of cries, but it was all one word: "Alleluia!"

CHAPTER SIXTEEN

Maddie marveled over and over that heaven was indescribably wonderful. Her senses couldn't take it in all at once. Instead, it was revealed slowly, with increasing glory—as though layers of film were continually being stripped from her eyes. She constantly noticed new details, colors for which she knew no name, exquisite sounds, and plants and animals as they had never been on earth. And the dazzling brightness of God covered it all. Maddie felt as though she were continually bathed in love.

Before the judgment began, Maddie and Daniel had the opportunity of wandering through the countryside. There, beside a sparkling stream where they had stopped to scoop handfuls of crystal-clear water, they found something neither one had ever dreamed of seeing. Maddie was sitting beside Daniel, holding his hand, enjoying his presence, and trying to take in the magnitude of beauty around her. An instant later, Jesus was sitting with them. But His arrival didn't startle Maddie. She simply felt a surge of happiness that He had joined them.

Maddie marveled at the sight of Him. He didn't look like the pictures painted by artists on earth. She found Him to be neither a humble, dusty carpenter nor a regal Victorian monarch. Instead, she found Him dignified and warm—Someone she felt instantly drawn to and unafraid of.

Jesus dipped His hand into the flowing spring, which stopped its flow instantly at His touch and became a still pool reflecting the blue dome of sky above. "Water," He said, "was one of My favorite illustrations on earth. Yet it never came close to expressing what I truly meant. The washing away of sins, for example." Here He paused to look directly at Daniel, His eyes soft but penetrating. "Your sins have been washed away, not in water but in My blood. But there is someone else here whose forgiveness you need."

Daniel understood what Jesus meant before Maddie did. She could see it in his eyes. The light in their brown depths leapt with wonder and excitement, but then clouded over with trepidation. "Is that possible?" he asked.

Jesus nodded and then placed an arm around Daniel's shoulders. "It is not only possible; it is necessary."

Daniel squared his shoulders, leaned against Jesus, and said, "If You'll help me, Lord, I can face this."

Then Randy Tilling appeared before them all—but a changed Randy Tilling. Maddie remembered him only as a man who had worked as a mechanic in Daniel's auto-repair shop. Maddie didn't know anything about his family. She didn't know anything about his life either. In fact, she didn't know anything about him at all, really—except the way he'd looked lying on the floor of the garage, his life's blood draining onto the cement as she frantically dialed 911 on the cell phone she'd wrested from Daniel's pocket after he'd passed out from drinking.

She'd gone to the shop that night to bring Daniel some supper. He often worked late, and she knew that while he was working, he was usually drinking. She never knew what kind of mood she'd find him in when he was under the influence.

That night, Randy's car had been parked outside, and Maddie knew there'd be trouble. The men had never gotten along. When she had heard their raised voices, she'd paused outside the door of the shop, trying to decide if she should leave the food there and go home or go in and see if her presence would calm the men. Before she could make up her mind, she heard their conversation.

"You've been stealing from me, and you admit it?" Daniel shouted, his words slurring and slow, his rage unquestionable.

"I have, and I'm almighty sorry about it too, boss," Randy said— though Daniel kept cutting him off with curses and there were loud crashes that made Maddie nearly jump out of her skin. It sounded as though in his anger, Daniel was throwing loose parts around the shop.

Randy tried to explain himself. "My wife—" he said, "she got religion. I thought it was all bunk, but there was something different. She changed, and I liked the way she changed. She didn't know it, but I started listening when the Bible people came to talk to her. I decided that if this Jesus fellow could change my wife so much, maybe He could change me too.

"And He did, I reckon, 'cause I knew I'd been doing wrong by you, taking money that didn't belong to me. I figured I needed it worse than you did, but it was still wrong. And I come tonight to tell you I'm sorry and to tell you I aim to pay back every red cent."

"Pay!" Daniel had screamed. "You'll pay all right!"

The gunshot came so suddenly and was so loud that Maddie had dropped the food onto the pavement and screamed. When she came to her senses and wrestled up enough courage to go inside, she'd found Daniel passed out across the hood of a car and Randy lying in a pool of blood. When the ambulance arrived, the attendants hadn't been able to revive Randy.

Now Randy was standing in front of them, more alive than he'd been on earth. His face was serene, and he was smiling. "Hello, Daniel," he said.

Maddie saw Daniel grip Jesus tightly. He reached out one hand towards Randy, his gesture both imploring and regretful. "I'm so very sorry," he sobbed. "Please forgive me."

Randy stepped forward, and the men embraced. "I have forgiven you," Randy assured Daniel. "It was the last thought I had; the last thing I remember passing through my mind before everything went blank."

The two men held each other for a long time, while Jesus and Maddie stood silently by. Then Maddie looked past Daniel and Randy to Jesus and caught His eye. "Thank You," she said. She could feel tears well up, but before they could spill, Jesus reached out once again and wiped them away. "Thank You," Maddie repeated, "for everything. For all this." She swept her hand towards the beauty around them. "For this too," she said, and she indicated Daniel and Randy. "For everything!"

"You are welcome," Jesus replied. "I'm so glad you chose to be here with Me. I've made a place especially for you."

"But Jesus, what of the people who aren't here? What of my son, my friends?" Maddie implored. "They made the wrong choice, but suppose they should regret it now? When we return to earth with You, what if they should change their minds and want to repent?"

Jesus' eyes held a sadness so deep and agonizing that Maddie began to cry. "How I wish that were the case," He said. "How I wish that one more opportunity would make the difference. If I tell you now that it wouldn't, you could doubt Me—"

"I wouldn't doubt You, Lord!" Maddie exclaimed passionately. "Never!"

"Nevertheless, you're uncertain. You're thinking perhaps those who weren't saved would change their minds if I gave them one more chance." Jesus paused and seemed to be seeing far into the future. "When we return to earth, the doors to the New Jerusalem will remain open for a time even as the throngs on earth prepare to attack. The open door will be an invitation to all who've had a change of heart. They will not be prevented from entering."

"Oh, Lord!" Maddie clasped her hands together and felt a surge of great joy.

However, her joy was short-lived. Jesus laid both hands on her shoulders and regarded her very solemnly. "They won't be prevented from entering," He repeated, and then, slowly and deliberately, added, "but they won't come."

"But—"

"I tell you this not because it is foreordained but because it is foreseen."

"You mean that You know they won't come even though they can because You know the future?" Maddie asked dully.

"Yes," Jesus said. "The Father and I have seen the events that will take place. But We can't alter them because We won't force people to be here against their will. Every created being will know and acknowledge that My Father is just and fair." Jesus put His arms around Maddie, and she wept softly into His shoulder.

"I want my son," she sobbed.

"I know," Jesus said sadly. "I do too."

When Maddie gained control of herself, she found Daniel and Randy in deep discussion. She would wait until later to tell Daniel what Jesus had said. Although she knew that extending to Brian the grace Jesus had given her was useless, she knew that she wouldn't feel right if she didn't try. If he didn't choose to join them, at least he could never doubt their overwhelming love for him.

Jesus had turned to Daniel. While He was talking, He reached over, lifted the crown from Randy's head, and turned it so that Randy could see the stars on it. Then He handed it to Randy and pointed out a star that flashed with fire like an opal. It looked exactly like a star on Maddie's crown. The name on the star was *Daniel*.

Randy's eyes filled with awe. "You were saved because of me?" he asked Daniel. "But how? I never witnessed to you or anybody. I was only a baby Christian when I died. You never even knew that I forgave you. As soon as you shot me, you passed out cold. I remember thinking how ironic it was that when you shot me, we both keeled over, like gunfighters in the old West who shot each other at the same time."

"But you did witness to me," Daniel protested, becoming animated. "For months after my arrest I couldn't get you out of my mind. I was sorry for what I'd done as soon as I was sober. But it was what you'd said to me—that you were sorry you'd stolen from me and you wanted to pay me back. I didn't understand why you'd risk everything to tell me that. And then your wife came to see me."

"In the jail?"

This was a detail even Maddie had never known. "I didn't tell you," Daniel told her, "because I was ashamed."

Daniel turned back to Randy. "She came to see me and to tell me she'd forgiven me. I cried like a baby. Here I'd done this terrible thing, and now your wife and kids didn't have a provider. I couldn't even provide for my own family, let alone yours, and the responsibility for all those helpless people ate at me day after day. *And yet they all forgave me.*

"The mental anguish I suffered was excruciating. I couldn't find relief anywhere. I asked Maddie to bring me a Bible, and I read it every second I had to spare. Later, I asked for a pastor to come and give me Bible studies. That's when I decided that whatever I had done, I was God's child, and I needed His grace and mercy.

"When I prayed for Him to take over what was left of the mess of my life, a feeling of peace like none I'd ever known before washed over me. Nothing had changed. I'd still committed murder. I was still responsible for the hurt I had caused by that action. And I was still in prison. But I wasn't under Satan's command anymore. I was following God. Nothing had changed except me, and that made all the difference."

THE THIRD COMING

Daniel reached his arm around Maddie's waist, and she leaned into him, her thoughts bittersweet. If only Brian had reacted to the truth the way Daniel had, she mused, they would all have been in heaven together. She mourned for their loss even as she rejoiced over all those who shared heaven with her.

BOOK TWO:
THE JUDGMENT

CHAPTER SEVENTEEN

In heaven, Maddie thought, time was a strange and mysterious thing. She didn't have any sense of its passage as she'd had on earth. The familiar markers were gone. There was no day and night, no rhythm of days filled with necessary chores—just an endless stretching of light. But she never felt bored or anxious or tired.

In the time before the judgment began, Maddie and Daniel visited with friends and family. So many people were there that joyful reunions took place constantly. During one lull, Maddie and Daniel were reclining on the soft grass that, Maddie noted, differed from earth grass in having a consistency soft as chenille. Lyn and Thomas were helping Redeemed learn how to walk. Back and forth he toddled over the lush grass, which, tickling his bare feet, drew loud laughter from him.

There was no way to tell his age, but Maddie figured that in earth time, he couldn't be more than a few weeks old. Yet already he was huge—nearly three feet tall! Each day he ate from the tree of life, and he seemed to grow before their very eyes. He had long, curly, golden hair that bounced as he walked unsteadily to the next set of outstretched hands. His features were all perfect. And his speech was already equal to that of a five-year-old earth child.

"How big did the angels say he would become?" Maddie asked again as she followed Redeemed with her eyes.

"Too big!" Lyn said, and she laughed. "My great, big, baby-giant." But she herself had grown as well, Maddie noticed suddenly. Then, looking around, she could see that they had all grown during their time in heaven. The change had been subtle, but Thomas, who was standing next to Jewel and speaking with great animation, now reached the angel's shoulder.

Jewel caught her eye and, seeming to divine her thoughts once again, gave her a nod as if to say, "See? I told you."

She laughed. "Yes," she replied though he hadn't spoken. "Yes, you did."

THE THIRD COMING

Maddie marveled again at how her ankle, a perpetual nuisance since she'd sprained it badly in high school, didn't protest with a stabbing pain as she shifted her position. Gone too were the scars on her arm from the time a horse threw her into barbed wire. And when she bent down to a pool of water, her reflection told her that even her wrinkles had been erased.

And she wasn't the only one who'd changed. They had all received perfect bodies at the Second Coming. In fact, she mused, the only blemishes she'd been able to find in all of heaven were the scars on Jesus' hands, feet, and side. They would never go away; they'd remain a constant reminder of the terrible price of sin.

"Mom?" Lyn was at her side, a worried look on her face. "What about Brian? What will happen to him?"

"I'm afraid Brian has made his choice." The words stuck in Maddie's throat like a handful of broken glass. She hated to think about that time at the end of the millennium when they would return to earth and the unrighteous dead would wake to their fate.

"But we can still try, can't we?" Lyn pleaded. "I *know* Bri. I know that if he just realized what it's like here, he'd change his mind. He'd want to be here with us. Can we still try?"

Maddie nodded. "We can try, honey; sure we can. If he doesn't decide to join us, at least he'll know how very much we love him and how we wish he could be with us."

"What will we do? How will we be able to let him know?"

"How about a banner?" Thomas suggested. "We could hang a big banner over the walls of the New Jerusalem when we return. It could say, 'We love you, Brian. Won't you come home?' or something like that. I'm not great with words."

Lyn choked down a sob. "Yes, you are," she said, her voice hoarse with emotion. "That's perfect. Come home, Brian; come home. I want us to be a family again—a whole family." She was silent, introspective for a while. Daniel leaned over and hugged her.

"I remember what it was like before you went to prison, Daddy," she said finally. "I remember how Brian and I used to play on the tire swing and wait for Mom to call us in to supper. We always watched for you. Whoever spotted you first was the king or queen until bedtime, and the other one was a stinky egg."

98

She giggled. "You would come in to read us bedtime stories. Brian was the oldest, so he claimed the top bunk, and I slept on the bottom one. But that meant you had to sit by my bedside when you read. I used to love the way you smelled of grease and Dove soap." Lyn broke down and began to cry. "Why did you have to leave us? Why?"

"Oh, honey, I'm so sorry. I'm so sorry," Daniel crooned, rocking Lyn back and forth while she cried. "I'm sorry for what I did and how it affected you. I was so selfish. I didn't think about anyone but myself in those days. If I could take it all back now, I sure would. Nobody and nothing would keep me from my family. You are all precious to me.

"My deepest sorrow is that because of my selfishness, I won't have the pleasure of spending eternity with my son. I never really knew him, and now I never will. He'll be lost to us forever. And I won't ever know what might have been if I hadn't been drinking; if I hadn't allowed my temper to rule my actions. If I'd been following Christ, how different it might all have turned out!"

Jewel stepped over and interrupted the conversation. "It's true that you cannot know how your decisions affected others. You do carry some responsibility for your son's rebellion. But the blood of Jesus, the Savior, covers all your sins. And Brian had to make a choice. Despite the influence of his circumstances, his choice was his own. Jesus gave all human beings the power to make the right choice and to stick with it. All they had to do was ask Him for it.

"When Brian chose to follow Satan, the rebel leader, he stepped out on his own. And although the circumstances in his life that were beyond his control influenced his choices, ultimately, the decision was his to make—and he chose the path of destruction. When angels approached him to present the truth, he ignored us. Though because of the prayers of others we constantly sought to guide him, he didn't acknowledge our presence. The chemicals he put in his body dulled his mind, and he could no longer distinguish between good and evil."

"But what if he hadn't been on drugs?" Maddie broke in to ask.

"He demonstrated by his actions before he started using the drugs that he wasn't interested in following the Savior. He was determined to get by on his own, through his own power and by his own wisdom. He abandoned Jesus and made his stand with Satan and his followers."

"Is that why he won't change his mind when we return to earth with the New Jerusalem?" Maddie asked.

The angel nodded his golden head. "He has made his final choice. His preferences are so much a part of him now that he can't separate himself from them—nor does he want to. He has sealed his own fate by his choices.

"But you can read all of this and much, much more in the books. The time even now approaches when you will sit upon your thrones with the Savior and go over these books page by page. Jesus has given you the solemn duty, responsibility, and privilege of reigning with Him."

Everyone was sober for a long time after the angel left. It wasn't until a legion of trumpets sounded from the golden city not far from where they stood, summoning them all, that they turned their thoughts away from those who weren't with them.

"I won't give up hope," Daniel said as they made their way toward the city. "As long as the doors are open, there is still a chance that Brian might change his mind."

"But you heard what Jesus and Jewel said," Maddie protested. "Although it is possible, it won't happen. You'll be bitterly disappointed when the time comes and Brian doesn't take advantage of his final chance. I love Brian as much as you do, but it is time to prepare our hearts to lose him for eternity."

"You don't understand. It's not that I believe he'll come back to us. I trust Jesus completely and know that what He says will happen. It's for my own sake that I keep hope alive—because if I don't act in faith, how could my faith ever be rewarded? If I don't step forward and believe, how would I ever know what might be? I owe it to Brian to believe in him until the end, bitter though that end will be for both of us. It's the last and only thing I can do for him now. I've failed him most of his life. Let me do this, at least."

Maddie put her arms around Daniel's waist and buried her head against his chest. "I don't want to lose my son," she cried.

"I know." Daniel smoothed her hair back from her forehead.

"Even that day when he held a gun to my head, I loved him. I would have loved him if he had shot me. I don't condone what he did. I don't even know half of it, but I love the Brian that is separate from the sin.

If only he would accept Jesus' help and wrench himself away from sin, he could be saved. It's his stubborn clinging to sin that is his ruin. How I hate sin and what it does to people! How I loathe what it did to my Savior! I am so very, very grateful that when it is gone, it will never rise again."

"So am I," a deep voice said so close to them that it made them jump. When Maddie looked up, she saw the tallest man she had seen yet. Beside him was a lovely woman, perfect in every way, about a head shorter than he. Without being told, she knew that they were Adam and Eve.

Adam spoke again. "We spent centuries regretting that through our actions, sin came into the world. With overwhelming grief, we witnessed the devastation it caused, and we wept as earth's beauty faded. When we woke to find that the promised Messiah had come and delivered us, we felt unspeakable joy."

"You lost a son too." Daniel's probe was gentle, but Maddie knew that he probed for a reason.

"As you have, I gather." Adam's great head bobbed with the admission. "Cain is the one the world knows about, but more followed his lead over the course of our lives. We watched many whom we loved turn away from the truth and the promise of redemption. It was a continual heartache for us."

"How do you bear it?" Maddie couldn't help asking.

Eve smiled, revealing perfect, white teeth. "We bear it, my dear, in the same way we bear every trial, every circumstance, every disappointment." She raised one long, bronzed arm and pointed toward the great throne in the middle of the city. It stood high above the rest of the city, and from it all light radiated. In the center of the light was God the Father, so bright that it was difficult to make out His shape.

Eve said, "We take our burdens to our Creator, and He carries them for us. We lean on Him, and He supports us.

"If we've learned one thing through this dark and troublesome time, it is that God loves us, cares for us, and wants the best for us. If we hadn't doubted Him, sin wouldn't have gained entrance to earth. No human being would have suffered, and our precious Christ wouldn't bear the scars of humanity's cruelty. What we could have had through faith, we have learned through incredible difficulty instead. How very glad we are that all was not in vain—that our Messiah prevailed and won for us eternal life in our beautiful garden of long ago."

Eve reached out and embraced Maddie before the pair walked with great strides toward the city, where multitudes now thronged. Daniel took Maddie's hand and squeezed it. Together, with Lyn, Thomas, and Redeemed, they made their way to the city to find out why they had been summoned.

BOOK TWO:
THE JUDGMENT

CHAPTER EIGHTEEN

Maddie always thought the accounts of God in the Bible were fearsome. The Bible writers had described God's physical appearance in ways that made no sense to her. They made Him seem alien and unfathomable, not like a loving Father. The Old Testament was full of wrath, and like others, she had been confused by the seeming contrast between God's harshness and punishments and Jesus' gentleness and forgiving spirit. In heaven, she found Them so alike that They seemed as one Being with two forms. She had eventually come to know God best and understand Him most by comparing His actions and words with Jesus' actions and words.

In reality, she discovered, God was like all the physical descriptions in the Bible put together, but more so. The accounts paled compared with the actual Being. She didn't have the words to describe Him, and she felt an empathy with the Bible writers when she ruefully considered how sadly their pens had failed them.

She also saw in God the Father's eyes an echo of Jesus' sadness when He spoke of those who were lost. Although the Father was awesome in stature and structure, she wasn't afraid of Him; rather, she felt herself worshipping Him and praising Him with shouts of gladness.

As the multitudes neared the city, angels came out and led them by the hand to golden thrones that had been set up in a courtyard. Row after row of them marched to the horizon. They were almost too dazzling to behold.

The angels led the saints to the thrones and invited them to be seated. Upon a platform, Jesus was seated at the right hand of God. A great crown graced His head, and His robes were dazzlingly white. The hem bore a band of red, as though it had been dipped in blood. The band signified Jesus' sacrifice.

Maddie sank gingerly onto her throne. The gold was polished to such a high degree that it seemed like liquid. She touched it with a tentative finger and found it solid and sleek. Her finger left no smudge. Slowly, she sat back and let her weight rest on the solid form of it. It was so comfortable that she felt as though she were reclining on a cloud. The arms of the throne were wide and carved like lion's paws at their ends. On one arm, someone had laid a beautiful Bible. Maddie cried out as she scooped it up.

In her hands was not her actual Bible, the one she had lost on earth, but one that looked just like it. In the precious, lost end pages, she found once again Daniel's tender note, written shortly after he'd become a Christian. Only the printing of the text differed from her old Bible. Inside were not the beloved, well-remembered words of her King James Version. Instead, artful gold letters she instinctively identified as Hebrew and Greek had been impressed upon each page. Maddie scanned them and realized with surprise that she understood them.

Not only could she read the Hebrew and Greek letters, but suddenly she also knew the meaning behind the words. It wasn't just that she comprehended the subtleties of language that had evaded her understanding before. It was far more than that. Normally, she would visualize a story as she read it. Now, as she read the words on the page, she could see in her mind's eye an entire recounting of not only the actual events but also of everything that went into the making of those events.

She "saw" the motives underlying each action, and she "knew" whether the actions were in harmony with the will of God. Everything that had cluttered her understanding before had disappeared. The Bible she held in her hands became a truly living book. She held it with awe and soaked up its words. For the first time in her life, she really understood why it was called the Word of God and how John could call Jesus "the Word" even though He was a person.

In addition to the text that consisted of the actual words written by the human authors, the inspiration was clearly visible, the meaning within the meaning. The "intent" as it had come from God, as well as the definition of each word and phrase, was easily understandable. Maddie found that she didn't have to grapple with the concepts or the language or content to understand the passages; they were plain to her. Questions she had often wondered about were answered without her even having to voice them.

She glanced over at Daniel and knew from the look of astonishment and wonder on his face that he was having a similar experience. Before she could ask him for his impressions, however, God began to "speak" to them. His words were not actual words. They were more like thoughts that impressed her mind, and she realized that everyone listening was impressed with the same words simultaneously.

As God spoke, in that same place in her mind's eye, she began to see events in history—before earth's history—in sequence. She saw Satan as he had once been, a beautiful angel in heaven—"the bright and shining star" of God, second only to Jesus. She saw his jealousy begin to take hold. She saw his rebellion, his whisperings, his subversion. Finally, she saw the war in heaven in all its fierceness. She "experienced" the agony of God, Jesus, the Holy Spirit, and the angels as they fought Satan and the rebelling angels and forced them out of heaven.

After that, earth's history began to unfold. She witnessed God's tender care of Adam and Eve in the Garden of Eden, and she saw Satan's vile influence, which ultimately destroyed the beauty and peace of the Garden and its inhabitants. As earth's history continued, a black cloud cloaked the planet, becoming darker with each passing year until God had to destroy most of the population through the Flood. Still, the evil hardly slowed at all, and soon the cloud was darker than before. When Jesus was killed on the cross, the blackness was impenetrable.

Maddie shuddered. She had no idea how long she'd been "watching" this accounting, how long God had been speaking, but it occurred to her suddenly that this was more than a retelling of history. It was a trial. But, unbelievably, she was not on trial. Nor were any of the others. She realized with a start that God was on trial here. He was giving the redeemed the privilege of judging Him in order to assure themselves that He had conducted Himself justly. He was answering Satan's accusations—letting the redeemed judge for themselves whether they were just or false.

Many would say that as the Creator, He wasn't obligated to explain His actions, methods, or motives to His creation. However, His love so far surpassed human expectations that He was not only willing but also eager to reveal Himself to them. Tears stung Maddie's eyes as she struggled to absorb the magnitude of a love so great that it had moved God to put Himself in such a vulnerable position. She staggered to her feet and shouted as loud as she could, "Praise God! Praise God!"

God's eyes were on her before the words were fully out of her mouth. Maddie felt as though, rather than being far, far away from her on a raised platform where all eyes could see Him, God stood before her. So she whispered the words again, for His ears alone: "Praise God; praise God."

God asked, "Why do you praise Me?" His voice matched hers in softness. The exchange was taking place between the two of them alone.

"Because You are just," Maddie answered simply.

"How do you know that I am just?"

Maddie thought a moment before replying. "A dishonest man hides his deeds or makes excuses for them. You neither excuse Yourself nor hide Your deeds. You simply ask us to judge You—a task for which we aren't qualified and to which we aren't entitled. In every possible way, You have worked to restore Your relationship with us when doing so wasn't even Your responsibility, because You didn't cause the initial rift. You have pursued us lovingly, and we have rejected You." Maddie began to cry softly as she recalled all the times when she had turned her back on what she now recognized as God's gentle wooing.

"You do not reject Me," God said.

"No," Maddie whispered. "Not now, but I have, in the past. I am so ashamed."

"There is no shame in love. You are forgiven."

Then God pointed to Jesus, whose countenance glowed as though He were on fire.

"My Son has paid the penalty for your sins. You may now enjoy the reward of His obedience."

"But I don't deserve it," Maddie wailed. As if in slow motion, Maddie saw her life pass before her eyes—and now she could see another dimension that had been hidden from her while she was on earth. Behind the scenes of her life, she vividly saw the spiritual warfare raging over her salvation. Each time she was obedient, the angelic forces rejoiced, but when she gave in to temptation, they grieved.

"If you deserved eternal life, you wouldn't have needed a Savior, and My Son and I wouldn't have had to be separated. But the penalty for sin is death, and only the death of a sinless One could pay that debt for eternity."

"Thank You," Maddie said. And then she choked and could say no more. Instantly, she felt God's arms around her, and she felt a warmth that made her tingle all over. It was as though with His embrace He erased the guilt and shame she felt and filled her with pure love and gratitude. She began to praise Him again, and when she did, she realized that her experience was not isolated. The multitude around her had apparently simultaneously had a revelation of their own lives and of God's vast love for them.

She joined them as they raised up their voices in unison to shout, "Alleluia! Salvation and glory and honor and power to the Lord our God! For true and righteous are His judgments! Amen! Alleluia! For the Lord God omnipotent reigns!"

BOOK TWO:
THE JUDGMENT

CHAPTER NINETEEN

After the judgment of God's people, which, as Maddie came to understand, was in actuality a judgment of the purity and completeness of Jesus' sacrifice, other books were opened, and in union with Jesus, the saints judged the wicked. As had been true of the redeemed, the motives of the wicked were open for inspection, and their deeds—even those they had tried to hide in darkness, the ones they thought no eye had seen nor ear heard—were laid open to the light of heaven.

The saints recoiled at the horrors they witnessed. But something surpassed this evil—the persistent and vehement rejection of the pleas of God's people as well as the spurned opportunities God had presented through angels and circumstances. The sinners had rejected opportunity after opportunity, until an impenetrable wall surrounded their hearts and remained there until their death.

The redeemed compared every deed with the statute book and the Bible. After each case, they were asked to judge whether God had acted uprightly. They were to determine if He was justified in deeming each soul beyond redemption. In case after case, they so determined. And after each such name and history in the book of death was recorded one desperately sad word: *Lost.* Beside that was noted the punishment Jesus and the saints apportioned to them.

Maddie began to feel a sense of desperation as she looked with foreboding to the time when Brian's case would come. Before she had time to think about it further, another name that she recognized arose: Jean King. Jean's deeds began to play out in the book before Maddie, who watched in dismay as she saw Jean change from a giving, loving, generous person who walked with God to a selfish, greedy, grasping person who allowed her own needs and desires to rule her life. The saints saw how she and her husband embezzled money from their employers, which they then converted into gold bullion and stockpiled in the safe in their bedroom and buried in several places in the woods. At the same time, Maddie and the others could see all the opportunities that had been lost for that money to further God's cause.

Originally, it was revealed, Jean and Ernie began stealing the money because they were concerned about the state of the economy and worried that no one would care for the less fortunate after the crash of the Social Security system. But their good motives couldn't override their evil actions. The more money they saved, the less inclined they were to use it to help anyone other than themselves. And as the state of the world declined, they used the money to maintain their comfort level and as leverage to protect themselves.

Maddie felt tears course down her cheeks as she saw Jean's lovely, bright, cheerful character warp and become stained and ugly. Yet, Jean still clung to the course she had chosen, refusing all the encouragement angels gave her to do the right thing by turning herself in. On the outside, she seemed the same person. But inside, she had become so hopelessly corrupted that nothing could penetrate the hardness of her heart, and the word *Lost* was written by her name.

Maddie reached out a hand to touch the image in the book, as if in that touch she could make Jean look outside herself and see what was really happening. But evil angels surrounded Jean, and she hid behind them, a hunted look on her face. She knew, Maddie realized. She knew what she was doing. She just made a different choice than the one Maddie and Daniel and Lyn had made.

"Why?" Maddie whispered. She couldn't comprehend it. Why would someone, *anyone*, choose temporary happiness and comfort over eternal happiness and heaven?

Jewel appeared at her side. "That has been the question through the ages. Why? Why did Lucifer strive to place himself above God? Pride took root in his heart, and he nurtured it. Sin was born, and it grew till it destroyed so many, many things."

"Why didn't God stop it before it started?"

"If He had, would we call Him just now? Would we say He gave people a choice? Or would we call Him a benevolent dictator? Could you love Someone who forced you to act as He pleased and not as you please?"

"The consequences," Maddie moaned softly. "The consequences were too high. They were too high for humanity, and they were too high for God. He would have saved Himself so much agony if He had prevented sin from happening."

Jewel smiled. "Yes. But in your words you have your answer. The cost of love *is* high. But the price was highest for God, and He paid it willingly. He didn't allow people to suffer alone. He gave the most, and He suffered the most."

"How do we know sin will never happen again? What assurance do we have?" Maddie asked, looking around her skeptically, as though sin might threaten them even there in heaven.

"We have the assurance of the Creator," Jewel said. "The Master saw that sin would come into existence. He laid out an escape route even before it occurred. He knew what it would cost to defeat it. The whole universe has been seeing the results of sin for these many centuries. Yet because you allowed the Master to cleanse your hearts and to live through you, you are safe to save.

"So, we know that sin will never reoccur because the Master says it won't. We are safe now. You and the others who were saved from the earth—you will bear witness to the terrible price of sin for eternity. If anyone asks you if sin was really as terrible as it seemed, you will be able to bear witness to them that it was much, much worse than it appeared."

Maddie nodded slowly. "I understand."

Jewel continued, "Human beings have suffered from the effects of sin, it is true. But they have experienced something that no one else has, not even angels."

"What is that?"

"A oneness with the Creator." He looked wistful. "The Master has dwelt in your heart. He carries humanity's scars and humanity's form forever."

The judgment continued, and Maddie concentrated on the names filing past. Eventually, they came to Brian's case, and his punishment was determined. Though she felt as if she'd been stabbed in the heart, Maddie couldn't disagree with his sentence or his punishment. God had acted fairly and given Brian opportunities long after human beings would have given up on him. Yet, though his name was recorded in the book of death, she still held the faint hope in her heart that he would change his mind when he realized, as all would, what Jesus had given up for all the world and for him alone.

When the judgment of the wicked was complete, the saints, along with Jesus, began to judge the fallen angels. Some words of the apostle Paul came to Maddie's mind that she'd never quite understood before: "Do you not know that we will judge angels?" Observing the beings in the books open before her, she found it hard to remember that the miserable creatures had ever had even a hint of the glory surrounding the angels who had kept the redeemed company since their arrival in heaven.

The fallen angels, pathetic beings that they were, resembled nothing so much as bedraggled bats. Their faces were coarse; their features degraded. Rather than standing tall and regal, as the other angels did, they shuffled in a stooped position, hunched into themselves from so many centuries of grasping and efforts at self-preservation. Their eyes, those windows of the soul, were shifty and restless—they never stopped roving the landscape for some poor, downtrodden soul to torment.

They had worked relentlessly to destroy any human in their path. While they respected no class, no pedigree, no circumstance, Christians brought out a particular type of antagonism in them. Their fierceness—and they could be fierce—rose to new heights when they worked to bring down a Christian. If they were able to make even one question his or her faith, they rejoiced and renewed their efforts. As Maddie and the other saints watched, they saw Satan attain victory after victory as he and his workers tirelessly attacked anyone who tried to follow the Master.

On earth, Maddie had been aware of the concept of spiritual warfare. She'd even read a few books on the subject, and she remembered one memorable sermon that had really opened her eyes. But she had never conceived of the ferocity of the attacks or the unending tirelessness of them. Nothing dissuaded the demons from their course. Nothing distracted them. Only when the angels of God stood in their path were they thwarted. Maddie could see the angels sent to protect the people of God when they prayed for protection or others prayed for them.

Over and above them all, God and Satan stood on opposite sides of the battlefield. Maddie could think of nothing else to call it. The wounded, dying, and dead lay all around, and few were the victors—those able to maintain their faith and their spiritual lives through the fray. These few glowed with a kind of light. They seemed calm amidst the chaos surrounding them.

It was then that a singular thought struck Maddie. In life, people had been so concerned with their physical state: their health, prosperity, and safety. Yet these were not the things that mattered in the end. God was fully able to protect His people, but His ultimate goal was not to protect them physically. The ultimate battle, the one He fought on a daily basis, was for their spiritual lives. Every other concern was temporary.

On earth, this had been a hard concept for Maddie to grasp as she made her way through her days, especially after Daniel's imprisonment. Life had become so difficult that it sometimes felt hopeless. The only thing she'd been able to cling to had been her faith and her assurance of salvation. Nothing else had been of such value. Now she could see the battle that had raged around her, constantly putting her at peril. And now, those fallen angels who had tormented her without mercy were before her for judgment.

Jesus and the saints judged each angel one by one, according to their deeds. When they were finished, the books closed with a loud crash—like the sealing of massive, steel prison doors. The saints turned their faces away from the books. As she did so, Maddie felt the enormity and finality of the judgment—something she'd been feeling intensely since it had begun—fall away from her. She was no longer sad, frustrated, or disappointed that people she desperately wanted to see in heaven, like Brian and Jean, weren't there. She was able to let go of her feelings. She could say with certainty that God was fair and just, and she knew without doubt that those who were not there could never have been happy there. For their own sakes, as well as for the sake of all the created beings, they couldn't live in heaven or on the new earth. God was giving heaven and earth a fresh start.

Then, from the throne, a voice like thunder proclaimed, "It is done. I am the Alpha and the Omega, the Beginning and the End. To him who is thirsty I will give to drink without cost from the spring of the water of life. He who overcomes will inherit all this, and I will be his God and he will be My son. But the cowardly, the unbelieving, the vile, the murderers, the sexually immoral, those who practice occult arts, the idolaters, and all liars—their place will be in the lake of burning sulfur. This is the second death." (See Revelation 21:6–8.)

Jesus now directed their gaze toward the New Jerusalem. It shone with the brilliance of the glory of God. Nestled on a hilltop of the greenest grass, it sparkled like a diamond against black velvet. Its great, high wall of jasper had twelve gates, three facing each direction, and an angel stood at each gate. On the gates were written the names of the twelve tribes of Israel. And on the twelve foundations of the wall, which were decorated with every kind of precious stone, were written the names of the twelve apostles of Jesus. The city itself was made of pure gold—even the streets, which were transparent, like glass, and laid out like a square. Unlike earthly Jerusalem, there was no temple in this city because the Lord God and His Son were its temple.

"Only those will enter this city whose names are written in the Lamb's book of life," Jewel said.

"Will we enter the city now?"

"Not now. First, we must return to earth, where the Master will finish what He started so long ago. He will destroy sin forever, and then eternity will begin without suffering or sadness or death." A wide smile lighted the angel's perfect features. "You have waited a long time for this moment, little sister."

Maddie's throat constricted, and she couldn't speak. Yes, she had waited a long time to live on a perfect earth. She reached out and took Daniel's hand on one side and Lyn's on the other. Redeemed, a fully grown man now and taller than Daniel, stood between them. And Thomas stood on Lyn's other side with his hand on her shoulder. Together, they turned to face Jesus, ready for the next step in their journey.

BOOK THREE:

THE END ... AND THE BEGINNING

BOOK THREE:
THE END . . . AND THE BEGINNING

CHAPTER TWENTY

The millennium was over. The time had arrived for God to wipe sin from the universe forever. Although Maddie knew that she and her family had spent a thousand years in heaven, she could hardly believe it. Time had ceased to have any meaning at all. It simply flowed, like water tumbling gently along a mountain stream. There'd been no agendas, no deadlines, no restrictions.

Now, however, the saints were about to retrace their journey of a thousand years ago. They were about to march to earth behind Jesus and a retinue of angels. The golden city would follow them to the place they had left under such dire circumstances so long ago. And now, for the first time since Maddie had come to heaven, she could sense anticipation crackling through the air.

When the journey began, she had no sense of movement—yet the host of the redeemed moved relentlessly forward through time and space. In what seemed like only moments but could have been a much longer period, they approached the small, dark planet that still spun aimlessly, carrying a load of death and destruction. It was the only blot in the entire universe—a black smudge on the glory of creation.

As they drew closer, Jesus suddenly shouted so loudly that Maddie felt the echo of His voice inside her, "Awake! Rise, and receive your doom!" And from their position near the middle of the throng, Maddie and her family began to see movement on the earth—a teeming, as if millions of ants were swarming a seashore.

"What is that?" Lyn asked. "Are those worms covering the earth?"

"They're people," Daniel answered. "Those are the wicked. We're still high up. When we descend more, you'll be able to see them more clearly."

As they drew nearer, they could see that Daniel was right. Not only did the shapes resolve into the figures of people, but they could even make out the condition of those who had just been raised. The saints Jesus had called from their graves in the first resurrection had risen immortally young, with perfect bodies. In contrast, the wicked now rose in relatively the same condition in which they had died—full of disease and bearing their injuries.

Stumbling, staggering, and shoving, they moved in whatever way they could toward the light of the Savior as He descended. Then, "Blessed is He who comes in the name of the Lord!" The shout from the wicked seemed to have been wrenched from their lips.

"Are they changing their minds?" Lyn wondered aloud.

"No," Daniel said, shaking his head sadly. "Look in their eyes. They're only admitting what is true. They feel exactly as they did when they died. See them—the way they glare at Jesus? They hate Him and all He stands for. But they have to admit that He is God."

As Jesus descended on the Mount of Olives, fragments of verses in Zechariah sprang unbidden into Maddie's mind. *"Then the LORD will go out and fight against those nations, as he fights in the day of battle. On that day his feet will stand on the Mount of Olives, east of Jerusalem. . . . Then the LORD my God will come, and all the holy ones with him"* (Zechariah 14:3–5, NIV).

"The prophecy," Lyn whispered excitedly, seeming to have remembered the very same verses, "it's coming true."

Maddie nodded. "Yes, it is."

Behind them, the Holy City, its brilliance an almost painful contrast to the dreariness of earth, came to rest on a spot that had been purified to receive it. Jesus lifted one scarred hand and motioned them all forward. And angels and saints together followed Him into the city.

"Now, Mom?" Lyn asked anxiously the moment their feet were touching the smooth transparent gold of the city streets.

"Now."

Without a word, Daniel, Thomas, and Redeemed followed Maddie and Lyn into one of the nearby houses. "What will we make it out of?" Thomas asked. But his question had already been answered. On the table, as if it were waiting for them, was a large sheet of a canvaslike material and big pens that looked like the markers they remembered using on earth. They quickly unrolled the material and smoothed the wrinkles.

Redeemed took a large red marker and held it aloft. "Can I write something?"

"Of course you can," said Lyn.

Redeemed bent his golden head and wrote, "We Love You, Uncle Brian," in an elegant cursive hand, though he'd never been to school of any kind.

Maddie took up a green marker, and when Redeemed was finished, she wrote, "Come Home, Son. I Love You. Mom."

Daniel chose blue and wrote, "I'm Sorry. Please Come Home. Love, Dad." And Lyn added her own message, her hand shaking.

When Thomas had drawn a border on their banner, they all stepped back to admire it critically. "Have we forgotten anything?" he asked.

Lyn shook her head.

Daniel wrapped his arm around Maddie's waist as they looked at the banner—their last loving gesture to their son. They knew their sentiments would not be reciprocated and probably not appreciated, but the love of the Savior filling their hearts gave them the strength to offer this message to Brian even though it would be entirely fruitless.

Lyn slipped into her parents' embrace and said, "I wish he were in here instead of out there."

"So do we," Daniel agreed. "So do we all."

Then, taking the banner, they made their way back outside and found a place where they could drape it over the wall. Other families, they now saw, had done the same. In fact, banners bearing heartbreaking messages covered the walls of the golden city.

They heard one mother pleading with her daughter, who was standing below, staring blankly up at her banner. "Please, Amelia," the woman said, "ask Jesus to forgive you. Come inside the Holy City." The daughter spat on the ground and walked away without even bothering to reply. As she left, she passed a gate to the city, which had remained open after the saints entered. She didn't spare it even a longing glance. Instead, she set her shoulders and marched out to where Satan appeared to be rallying his troops.

"What are they doing out there?" Lyn asked, peering at the frenzied activity.

"They're getting ready for battle," Thomas said. He didn't appear to be afraid of this prospect, but Maddie felt a shiver run through her.

"Who are they going to fight? Us?"

"That's what they think," Thomas replied. "Many of those men were great warriors and generals and leaders. It's likely that many of them died in the midst of battle, and they've just been raised to life again. Do you think they've changed at all?"

"No." Daniel's voice was soft. "And I could have been one of them. Praise God for His infinite mercy and kindness."

Then the voice of Satan floated up on the air. It carried to every part of the city. "We've been wronged!" Satan was shouting. "We've been cheated! But no longer. I'm here to help you win back your rightful inheritance. I've raised all of you from death to help me. I've broken your chains. I've given you new life."

He paced back and forth—a formidable figure, if a debauched one. "This world is *my* inheritance!" He thumped his chest with a fist. "It was given to me, and a usurper is trying to wrest it from me. But I tell you this: When I have prevailed over Him and His followers, we will make them our slaves. They will serve us, their rightful masters.

"Do you see their city? It's insignificant compared to what I will build for you as my subjects. You won't live together in one small city. Each of you will be master of his own city."

Satan paused to let this sink in before he continued. "There are untold treasures hidden within that city—treasures they've taken from us unlawfully. All we have to do is take them back. The enemy forces are few, and we are many. We have the best military minds in the world here to help us. We'll never have a better opportunity to overcome them than we do at this moment—before they have a chance to organize themselves. We can quickly form battalions and march on the city. We'll slay them before they know what has hit them.

"If we don't conquer them, their Leader will enslave us all. He is a most cruel master. The throne on which He sits is rightfully mine, and I'm going to claim it. You must choose. Are you for us or against us?"

The multitude before Satan was so vast that Maddie couldn't even hazard a guess as to how many it numbered. In the throng, she saw men who towered over the others—men she presumed to have lived during the time before the Flood. The multitude formed a vast and powerful army that was made more menacing because it was led by some of the most superior military minds earth had ever produced.

As Maddie's eyes roamed over the faces below her, faces full of unmitigated hatred, she suddenly noticed one that stood out. Daniel's grip on her arm tightened as he followed her gaze. "Brian!" they shouted together. And when Lyn realized they had spotted her brother, she added her voice to theirs.

In that vast multitude, across such a distance, there was no earthly way Brian could have heard them. Yet his eyes shifted suddenly, as if something were pulling them to where his family stood on the wall.

"Brian!" they called again. "We love you!"

Brian's face filled with such fury that Maddie was suddenly reminded of the day he held a gun to her head and threatened to shoot her. "Leave me alone!" he shrieked. "You don't love me. You never have. You never once helped me when I was desperate, so don't try to act as if you love me now. I won't buy it."

"Brian, come home with us. Repent. Jesus will forgive you. Come into the city while the gates are still open. Soon it will be too late."

Maddie could hardly force the words from her throat, it was so tight. But even as she uttered them, she knew it was no use. Brian was the same today as he had been the last day she'd seen him alive. He was full of hatred, cunning, and deception. He had always blamed others for his failings, and he hadn't changed.

"Ha!" Brian threw back his head and roared with laughter. "Weren't you listening? We'll be in your precious city soon enough, and you'll wish we weren't. If you think you can make things easier on yourselves by trying to get on my good side now, you're mistaken. I don't care about you. I don't care about any of you." He screamed the last words so loudly that the veins in his neck bulged, and spittle flew from his mouth. Then, very deliberately, he turned his back on them.

CHAPTER TWENTY-ONE

The camp of the wicked buzzed with relentless movement. When Maddie watched the bustling activity from the wall of the New Jerusalem, she could see Satan conferring with his angels and with military officers she'd read about in history books. It was clear that not only were they preparing for victory, they were expecting it. This was no slapdash army that they were creating. It was the epitome of precision and ruthlessness.

Troops marched across the vast plains surrounding the city, drilling constantly. And factories were constructed, seemingly from nothing, to make the weapons the troops would carry with them into war. Their morale was high. At times, Satan lost control, and groups of them rushed the city—only to turn back after throwing grenades. As they retreated, they hurled insults at the inhabitants of the city, who watched solemnly from the wall.

Meanwhile, the redeemed conversed with angels, decorated their houses, and planted small, exquisite gardens beside them. They worshiped God and studied with Him the mysteries never before revealed to humankind. Inside the city, you would never have known that darkness existed beyond the protecting walls. The presence of God illuminated everything, and the saints basked in His light continually.

After a time, Maddie could only guess how long, activity in the camp of the wicked became frenzied and began to take on the aspect of finality. Massive groups of soldiers began to form up, each with its own leader and its own job. Satan could be seen every day pacing before them, shouting instruction and stirring them up.

He was so persuasive that it wasn't difficult to see why the masses gathered before him, soaking up every word and following every suggestion. He appealed to their base natures, focusing their attention on the city before them and its desirability even though it didn't rightfully belong to them. If God wouldn't give it to them, Satan said, he would lead them, and they would take it. Maddie marveled at how Satan worked the crowd. In the same way that he had convinced millions on earth to follow him in the past, he now persuaded them again—*even after they could plainly see the results of their base decisions.*

"They just don't realize what they're doing," she murmured to herself.

"They realize it," said Daniel, who came up to stand beside her at the wall. "It's just that their own selfishness and pride are too strong for them to fight any longer. They can't do it on their own. None of us ever could. But they were never willing to let God purge them of self, so now self is all they have."

"But what has it gotten them?" Maddie cried, waving her hand at the masses of the wicked. "Look at them. They have no comfort, no hope, and no love. They don't even have a roof over their head. They have, literally, nothing—nothing but the hatred they cling to so stubbornly. Don't they feel how lost they are; how deprived?"

Daniel shook his head. "No. I don't believe they do. But even if they did, they're confident that they can just take whatever they're missing from someone who has it. Us, for instance. They want this city, and they want revenge on us, and those desires are driving them. But they don't see that there is no end to the evil they've embraced. Not a single one of them is safe from another. In a place where everyone looks out for himself or herself, no one is ever truly safe."

Maddie pondered this for a moment. Then she asked, "Have you seen Brian lately?"

"No, not since he walked away from us."

"I think about him. I wonder if he thinks of us."

Daniel took her by the shoulders. "Brian had choices just like the rest of us," he said. "It could just as easily have been any of us outside these walls. But we threw ourselves on the mercy, love, and goodness of Jesus. Brian didn't make that choice. He chose himself. He doesn't want to be here. Nothing—no amount of time, no number of opportunities—can make his heart change if he doesn't want it to."

Maddie let Daniel pull her into a soothing embrace. "I know," she whispered against his shoulder. "It's just that I want so much for him to be here."

"Me too," Daniel said. "Me too. But God allowed each of us to make our own choices, and we have to do that too. Brian didn't want to be here—that's why he's not here."

As they stood together beside the wall, a loud roar—like the scream of a tornado—pierced the air. Looking down, they saw the armies that had amassed on the plains below suddenly swarm toward the city, with Satan leading them.

"Close the gates," Jesus said with authority from His throne. Angels immediately went to the massive city gates and pulled them shut.

The inhabitants of the city looked over the wall at the onrushing hordes. Compassion was written on every countenance, and there was no sign of fear or doubt that they would be safe and that Jesus would triumph over Satan.

As the armies of Satan surrounded the city, the throne of Jesus began to rise above the city, and the inhabitants of the city rose with it. Maddie and Daniel clasped hands as they rose in company with the redeemed to stand beside their King. Jesus had never looked so majestic and powerful as He did at that moment. God's glory surrounded Him and poured out through the city and beyond, flooding the entire earth.

With the rest of the redeemed, Maddie and Daniel sang, "Salvation to our God who sits on the throne and to His Son." The angels and the seraphim joined them, and Maddie felt she would burst with the joy of their song. This was the moment all heaven had anticipated with greatest pleasure. Jesus was to receive His final coronation. A glittering, bejeweled crown was placed on His head and the tables of the divine law in His hands. Now He was invested with the authority to conduct the judgment of the wicked.

The record books the redeemed had examined in heaven were opened once again. But the wicked didn't need to see the record of their deeds written there, for as soon as Jesus' eye rested upon them, they knew full well every sin they had committed. The conviction they felt was written plainly on their faces. They didn't need to utter a word to confirm it.

Then, a cross appeared above the throne, and images from the beginning of the world and the fall of Adam and Eve through the plan of redemption and the birth, life, and death of Jesus all played out before the entire earth. So vivid was the spectacle that Maddie could almost believe it was happening all over again. But one look below, at the stunned faces of Satan and his followers, reminded her that they were viewing history. Sin would never again enter the world; Satan would have no further power to do evil. The saints, with one voice, threw their crowns at the feet of Jesus and exclaimed with thankful hearts, "He died for me!"

Turning from this scene of great rejoicing, Maddie watched the faces of the wicked as they gazed at the tables Jesus held in His hands. In their eyes dawned the light of realization as they were forced to acknowledge that the rules they had despised in life were truly meant for the happiness of all created beings. As the songs of the redeemed swept over the plains, the wicked raised their voices and proclaimed with all of heaven, "Great and marvelous are Your works, Lord God Almighty; just and true are Your ways, King of saints!" Even Satan acknowledged the justice of his sentence, bowing low before God. "Who shall not fear You, O Lord, and glorify Your name? For You only are holy; for all nations will come and worship before You; for Your judgments are made manifest."

In contrast, Satan, stripped of all bravado and cunning, appeared as he truly was: weak, pathetic, and scheming. For the first time the wicked saw clearly through his deception, and all creatures on earth despised him for leading them into rebellion. His own works, now revealed in their entirety, condemned him.

However, this revelation prompted no sign of repentance or contrition from Satan. Instead, he rushed into the assembled armies and made one last effort to stir up the wicked against God. But Satan's time of influence and power was over. The multitude saw through his charade, and they turned on him savagely.

As the assembly of the wicked descended into a seething mass of hatred and rage, the saints descended into the city. From Maddie's position near the wall, she saw the entire surface of the earth become a molten mass. It stretched as far as the eye could see—an endless ocean of fire that was consuming the wicked. Some were destroyed instantly; some burned longer. She knew each was being punished according to his or her deeds. Satan burned the longest, not only for his own sins but also in punishment for all the sins he had encouraged others to commit. "Sin cannot exist in the presence of God," Jewel had explained to them earlier. "Because the wicked will not relinquish it, they must perish."

The roar of the flames slowly died down as, at last, all the sinners, and finally, even Satan, were destroyed. A calm stillness fell upon the cleansed planet. For the first time in seven thousand years, the earth and all its inhabitants were at rest—one with the Creator. And, spontaneously, the righteous broke into a song of praise: "Alleluia: for the Lord God omnipotent reigns!"

BOOK THREE:
THE END . . . AND THE BEGINNING

CHAPTER TWENTY-TWO

Maddie coaxed a tender vine around the base of a sturdy tree she'd planted to celebrate the completion of their heavenly home. The tree's green leaves danced and swayed, making a beautiful tinkling sound, like many bells, as they brushed together. The melody filled Maddie's heart with joy, and she stopped to sing a song of praise to the Savior for His sacrifice on her behalf.

"Mom!" Lyn's voice rang through the crystal air as she bounded around the corner of the house with Redeemed following her, delight and wonder on his beautiful face. "Guess what!"

Maddie turned to greet her child and grandchild. The dark days of earth, behind them now, only rarely entered her mind. Those days of doubt when Lyn was in rebellion, pregnant and scared, hadn't been erased from her mind, but they no longer gripped her the way they once had. She still occasionally spoke of them, when beings from other planets asked her about what her life was like in the old days. Now, when she looked at Lyn and Redeemed, she felt an overwhelming sense of gratefulness that they were with her and Daniel in the earth made new.

"Did Redeemed find another new animal?" she teased. It was his favorite game, locating all the species of animals on the planet. He had a natural way with them, and his own house, built not far from Maddie and Daniel's and Lyn and Thomas's, had frequent guests of the four-legged or winged variety.

"No," Lyn said, her voice hardly able to contain her excitement. "We're going on a trip. All of us."

"Oh? Where are we going?" Trips between the worlds, something scientists on earth had only dreamed about, were a fairly common occurrence in the new age. They simply thought themselves to their destination, and in that instant, they arrived. There was no danger of plane crashes or train derailments or car accidents. Travel was safe at last.

"Guess!" Lyn said, her eyes twinkling.

CHAPTER TWENTY-TWO

They had already visited many of the more popular planets, so Maddie knew she couldn't choose one of them. "Are we going to Straitha?" she guessed, settling on a universe that few had yet visited.

"No, try harder, Grandma!" Redeemed could hardly contain himself.

"What's the boy doing now?" Daniel asked as he came around the corner of the house, carrying a chunk of diamond he had been smoothing to fit into a window for Lyn's house.

Maddie laughed. The "boy" was a head taller than Daniel and closing in on twelve hundred years old. But he was still so full of childish wonders at all the delights of heaven that he did, in a way, seem young. Maddie constantly marveled again at Redeemed's innocence. He was one of the few humans on the new earth who had not actually grown up in the old earth, having been born just before Jesus came to rescue them. Now, he was tall, more than twelve feet tall, and perfectly proportioned, with features that a master sculptor might have carved from the finest alabaster.

"Where are we going?" Daniel asked again.

"That's what Grandma's been trying to guess," Redeemed said.

"And not succeeding," Maddie laughed.

"We're going to Orion's belt!" Redeemed finally blurted out, unable to contain himself any longer.

Daniel's brow furrowed in puzzlement. "Orion's belt? You mean we're going to heaven?"

"Not just to heaven, Daddy," Lyn said. "We're going on a camping trip. With Jesus!"

"Jesus invited us to go camping with Him," Redeemed repeated excitedly. "In heaven!"

Maddie felt her heart leap in her chest. What a wonderful opportunity! What a privilege!

"How exciting!" Maddie exclaimed, joining her family in a jubilant group hug. Her heart was filled almost to overflowing. Every time it seemed impossible for more happiness to fit inside it, her heart stretched to accommodate even more. "Alleluia!" she shouted. And Daniel, Redeemed, and Lyn echoed her shout.

Just then, they saw Jesus smiling at them as He walked across the valley toward them. "Thank You," Maddie whispered.

THE THIRD COMING

Jesus' voice came back in her ear alone. "You are very welcome, my daughter."

Then, speaking to them all, He said, "I have loved you with an everlasting love; I have drawn you with loving-kindness. Come, let us fellowship together."

*   *   *   *   *

The Spirit and the bride say, "Come!"
And let him who hears say, "Come!"
Whoever is thirsty, let him come;
and whoever wishes,
let him take the free gift of the water of life."
Revelation 22:17, NIV

BIBLIOGRAPHY

Hegstad, Roland. "Who Said Judgment Is Bad News?" *Adventist Review* (North American Division Edition), March 3, 2005, 30–33.

Maxwell, Graham. "The Final End of Sin and Sinners"—a series of three audio tapes dated January 21, 1995.

White, Ellen G. *The Great Controversy.* Nampa, Idaho: Pacific Press®, 1941.

IF YOU'VE BEEN INSPIRED BY THIS BOOK, YOU'LL ALSO ENJOY THE PRAYER WARRIORS TRILOGY

by *Céleste Perrino-Walker:*
Prayer Warriors Trilogy

Book One: **Prayer Warriors**

As powers of darkness threaten God's people in the last days of earth's history, angels of light gather around their human charges. Armed with the most potent weapon of all—prayer—God's faithful few struggle to keep their eyes on the Savior and eternal life.

0-8163-1359-8. Paperback
US$12.99, Can$19.49.

Book Two: **Guardians**

The power of prayer comes to life in this gripping drama. Observe the scenes of spiritual warfare where humans struggle with life as they are influenced by angels and demons. *Guardians* will change you, the way you see the world, and the way you pray.

0-1863-1407-1. Paperback.
US$12.99, Can$19.49.

Book Three: **Prayer Warriors, The Final Chapter**

This final book of the series gives behind-the-scenes glimpses of angelic activity initiated by the prayers of their charges. This is a gripping story of the power of prayer.

0-8163-2001-2. Paperback.
US$12.99, Can$19.49.

Order from your ABC by calling 1-800-765-6955, or get online and shop our virtual store at <www.AdventistBookCenter.com>.

- Read a chapter from your favorite book
- Order online
- Sign up for email notices on new products